The Mormon Image in Literature

The Mormon Image in Literature reprints important literary works by and about Mormons—from the sensational anti-polygamy books and dime novels of the Civil War era to the first attempts of Mormon writers to craft a regional literature in their Great Basin kingdom. Each volume contains a critical introduction, helpful annotations, and multiple appendices that enlighten and enliven the text. These volumes have been designed for both Mormon and non-Mormon readers who want to understand the cultural importance of Mormonism during the first Latter-day Saint century.

Current and forthcoming titles in
THE MORMON IMAGE IN LITERATURE series:

CLAUDINE LAVALLE;

OR,

THE FIRST CONVICT.

THE MORMONESS;

OR,

THE TRIALS OF MARY MAVERICK.

BY

PROFESSOR JOHN RUSSELL,

OF BLUFFDALE

ALTON:

COURIER STEAM PRESS PRINT.

1853.

THE MORMONESS;

OR, THE

TRIALS OF MARY MAVERICK.

A NARRATIVE OF REAL EVENTS.

CHAPTER I.

"Delusion! ah! the *weak* may be deluded;
But is the learned, the enlightened, noble Varus,
The victim of delusion?—It cannot be!
I'll not believe it."—*The Martyr.*

"*Halloo! Halloo!*" uttered in the loudest tones of the human voice, instantly brought the little family of James Maverick to the door. At the gate was the well-known son of a neighbor, mounted upon a shaggy, half-broken colt, which he was fond of riding because it was his own. The animal seemed resolved, by his rearing and pitching, of which the boy was not a little proud, to give his rider no opportunity of performing his errand. But, at length, with many interruptions, intermingled with the frequent cry of "who-a! who-a, Tecumseh," the message was delivered, and the youth and his steed were on their way to the next neighbor's, to deliver there the same tidings.

That young man was the son of Deacon Hezekiah Cobb, a worthy old farmer of that settlement, whose house was known far and near to the religious community by the expressive name of "*Pilgrim's Tavern.*" Not only preachers of the gospel, but professors of religion of every stripe, found a welcome under his hospitable roof. The very sight of his well-filled barn often made the veriest "*backslider*" devout. Many and many a church member, seldom suspected, at home, of being righteous overmuch, has driven his weary horses ten miles beyond a tavern to put up for the night with the good deacon, rather than stay with "the people of the world."

He had sent his son to acquaint the inhabitants of the settlement, far and near, that a Mormon had arrived at his house, and would preach in the school-house that night, at early candle light.

5

THE MORMONESS;

OR, THE

TRIALS OF MARY MAVERICK

A NARRATIVE OF REAL EVENTS

by

John Russell

1853

Edited and Annotated by

Michael Austin

and Ardis E. Parshall

SALT LAKE CITY, 2016
GREG KOFFORD BOOKS

Published in the USA.

ISBN 978-1-58958-507-2 (paperback)
Also available in ebook.

Greg Kofford Books
P.O. Box 1362
Draper, UT 84020
www.gregkofford.com

2020   19   18   17   16   5   4   3   2   .
_____

Library of Congress Control Number: 2015960363

Contents

**The Mormoness; or, The Trials of Mary Maverick:
A Narrative of Real Events**

Appendix A:

Appendix B:

Appendix C:

John Russell of Bluffdale
and the Trials of Mary Maverick

In his famous *Autobiography*, Parley P. Pratt recalls that he and fellow missionary William E. McLellin faced considerable opposition from Baptist ministers when they started preaching in Green County, Illinois in the winter of 1833. He reports that a preacher named "Dotson" took great offense to the Book of Mormon and "opposed us with much zeal . . . both in public and in private, and from house to house." John Mason Peck, perhaps the most famous Baptist in Illinois, engaged them in lengthy disputes designed to humiliate them.[1]

But one of the Illinois Baptists was different from the others. Pratt reports that "a Baptist minister by the name of John Russell, a very learned and influential man, invited us to tarry in the neighborhood and continue to preach." He continues that Russell "said that his house should be our home, and he called a vote of the people whether they wished us to preach more. The vote was unanimous in the affirmative."[2] This generosity of mind and spirit was typical of the man who extended it. John Russell was one of the most formidable educators, editors, and writers of Western Illinois during the first half of the nineteenth century. But he was also famous for his open mind and his willingness to defend those whom others had determined to attack.

Born and educated in Vermont, Russell came to the frontier with his family at a time when "going West" was simply what young people did if they wanted opportunities for advancement. After graduating from Vermont's Middlebury College in 1817,

---

1. Parley P. Pratt, *Autobiography of Parley P. Pratt*, 6th ed. (Salt Lake City: Deseret Book, 1966), 84–92. "Dotson" is almost certainly "Elijah Dobson," a local Baptist leader and friend of John Russell. It was Dobson who signed Russell's license to preach the same year.

2. Ibid., 84.

Russell first went South to teach classics, literature, and modern languages in Georgia. He soon left that position, however, when it became apparent that his anti-slavery views were incompatible with the community he served. He spent eight years in the St. Louis area as a teacher and private tutor before settling permanently with his family in Illinois in 1828. He purchased land in Green County that he called "Bluffdale," which eventually became the name of the surrounding town. The town merged with the man, and, for the rest of his life he wrote and interacted with people as "John Russell of Bluffdale."

We know from their letters to each other that both Russell and his wife Laura were impressed with Pratt and not entirely opposed to Mormonism in its earliest incarnation. In April of 1833, John wrote Laura from nearby Alton to tell her that "Mormonism is the main theme of inquiry" and that "[i]t was circulated in this region that I had joined them." He went on to say that several of his acquaintances "said it was actually a fact that I had been baptized and joined. . . . I have said nothing against either them or any one else, and so you must hear no fears that I have said anything hard, as I know you would have."[3] A year later, in another letter, Laura told John that "Mr. Pratt has been in Bluffdale again, accompanied with an Elder by the name of White, a very smart man." She commended both their preaching and their understanding of scripture and closed the letter with the observation that "the Mormonites preach some truths that sink with weight on my mind. If it is (as some affirm) fanaticism I like to hear it."[4]

No member of the Russell family ever joined the Church of Jesus Christ of Latter-day Saints, but they continued to receive Mormon missionaries cordially whenever they passed through Green County. When the Saints were expelled from Missouri, a

---

3. John Russell to Laura Ann Russell, April 27, 1833. John Russell and Family Papers, 1792–1927, box 1, folder 4. Abraham Lincoln Presidential Library and Museum, Springfield, Illinois.

4. Laura Russell to John Russell, Bluffdale, January 5, 1834. John Russell and Family Papers, box 1, folder 4.

number of Latter-day Saints, including Pratt and Sidney Rigdon, took refuge in the Russell's home, and it was from them, his son later wrote, that John heard "the heartrending stories and barbarity of the cut-throat Missourians." One of these stories in particular stayed with Russell for a long time: the story of the Merrick family—Levi Merrick and his nine-year-old son Charley, who were killed by the mob that attacked Haun's Mill in October of 1838, and Philinda Clark Eldredge Merrick, the Mormon mother who watched as her husband and son were murdered for their beliefs.[5] Fifteen years later, Russell would imagine the life of Philinda Merrick before and after Haun's Mill as he wrote one of the first fictional accounts of Mormonism in American history.

Long before writing *The Mormoness*, Russell tried to use his influence to help the Latter-day Saints in Illinois. One of his most frequent correspondents in the 1830s and 1840s was Thomas Gregg, a prominent journalist who was associated with the *Warsaw Signal*—a Hancock County newspaper that adopted a harsh anti-Mormon tone in 1841 under the editorship of Thomas Sharp. In a letter to Gregg dated July 7, 1841 (see Appendix B), Russell took great exception to the *Signal's* anti-Mormon editorial policy. "I do not believe that it is your intention to excite a mob against these deluded fanatics," he wrote to his friend, "but you could not pursue a more direct course to affect that object, if such <u>was</u> your design."

Even as he made it clear that he rejected the Mormons' theology and their claims of revelation, Russell devoted seven hand-written pages to criticizing the paper's rhetoric. Russell criticized what he saw as two major flaws in the paper's position. First, he insisted that American citizens had the right to be wrong in religious matters without being subjected to violent attacks. "Joe Smith is an American citizen," he lamented, "and shame on the people—all that can tamely stand by and see the sacred rights of any American cloven down."

---

5. Spencer G. Russell, "John Russell of Bluffdale, Illinois," *Transactions of the Illinois Historical Society* 6 (1901): 103–7.

Russell also argued that the *Signal* would end up strengthening Mormonism by causing it to be persecuted and, thereby, validated. Speaking of Nauvoo, he wrote, "I have not a doubt but that the Signal will destroy the settlement and town of the Mormons. I am fearful that on opening the next number I shall see that event announced in starring capitals." But he also felt that "the excitement will soon fade away and the deepest feelings of sympathy be awakened for that people. Their errors will all be forgotten in their sufferings."[6]

A year later, when Gregg took over publication of the *Signal* from Sharp, he did substantially moderate the paper's editorial policy towards the Mormons, though there is no way of knowing what, if any, influence Russell's letter had on that decision.

John Russell the Writer

Like many educated people of his day, John Russell could not completely support himself and his family as a writer, an editor, a teacher, a minister, or a public intellectual—so he pieced together a livelihood combining all of these vocations into a single career. Twice after moving to Bluffdale, he left home for extended periods of time to take positions as a newspaper editor in Kentucky (1841–1842) and a school master in Louisiana (1843–1849), which meant that he was away from Illinois during most of the time that the Mormons were in Nauvoo. For two years (1837–1839), he edited his own newspaper called *The Backwoodsman*, based in Grafton, Illinois. And for the entire time that he lived in Bluffdale, his income was supplemented by his position as the local postmaster.

More than most frontier intellectuals, however, Russell was able to earn a good portion of his income by writing for local publications. He wrote his first book when he was only nineteen years old—a historical work called *The Authentic History of the Vermont State's Prison* (1812), which was commissioned by the state government to comply with a federal law. In his introduc-

---

6. John Russell to Thomas Gregg, Bluffdale, 7 July 1841. John Russell and Family Papers, box 1, folder 6.

tion, Russell acknowledged that his only motivation for writing the book was "the aid that the sale of the copyright would afford the author in obtaining a collegial education."[7] And it worked. The money that he earned from the book allowed him to begin studies at Middlebury College in 1814 and launched him in his career as a man of letters.

Russell contributed many pieces of fiction and nonfiction to the frontier presses in Missouri and Illinois, including novels, novellas, and at least one extended work of comparative theology. However, throughout his life, he was known as a writer, primarily as the author of "The Venomous Worm"—a 450-word cautionary message about the evils of alcohol, published in a Missouri newspaper sometime between 1819 and 1821. In 1838, this obscure little parable was included in the first edition of the fourth grade *McGuffey Reader*. For the next fifty years, nearly everybody in the United States who made it to the fourth grade read at least one work by John Russell of Bluffdale. Nearly fifty years after Russell's death, it was reprinted by the Illinois State Historical Society in its official journal, with the following preface: "The Secretary of the Illinois State Historical Society has had many requests from interested persons for copies of 'The Venomous Worm,' which is perhaps the most famous of Prof. John Russell's writings. We accordingly reprint it in order that it may be easily accessible to interested persons."[8]

The bulk of Russell's fiction was written for three different kinds of publications in three roughly defined periods of his life. Between 1833 and 1836, he wrote a group of short stories for the *Western Monthly Magazine, and Literary Journal*, a historical-literary journal published by Judge James Hall and centered in Vandalia, Illinois.[9] In the early 1850s, he published several works of fiction in the

---

7. *The Authentic History of the Vermont State's Prison* (Wright and Sibley Printers, 1812), unpaginated introductory material.

8. John Russell, "The Venomous Worm," *Journal of the Illinois State Historical Society* 4, no. 3 (October 1911): 349–50.

9. Frank L. Mott, *A History of American Magazines* (Cambridge: Harvard University Press, 1938), 595–98.

Alton Courier in nearby Alton, Illinois. And in the late 1850s he wrote a number of stories and novellas with religious themes for the American Baptist Publication Society of Philadelphia.

The Mormoness, or, the Trials of Mary Maverick belongs to this middle group of works. It was originally published in six installments in the *Alton Courier* in August and September of 1853. As soon as it finished its run, it was combined with another of Russell's serials called *Claudine Lavalle, or, The First Convict* and published in book form by the *Courier's* press.[10] When published in this form, *The Mormoness* became arguably the first, and undoubtedly one of the most important fictional accounts of the Mormons by somebody who had been a witness to their struggles.

The Trials of Mary Maverick

We can call *The Mormoness, or, The Trials of Mary Maverick* "the first novel to treat Mormonism" only with two important qualifications. In the first place, it is not quite a novel. At about 25,000 words, it is better described as a novella, though very few Americans in 1853 would have known or cared much about the difference. And it is not quite the first sustained work of fiction about Mormons. That designation goes to a book written ten years earlier: *Monsieur Violet* (1843) by the British adventure writer Frederick Marrayat, which incorporates a visit to Nauvoo in its main character's sprawling odyssey across the American West.[11]

---

10. John Russell, *Claudine Lavalle, or, The First Convict; [and] The Mormoness, or, The Trials of Mary Maverick* (Alton [Ill.]: Courier Steam Press, 1853). It is likely that Russell wrote *Claudine Lavalle* specifically for this volume. It is the only one of his longer works whose handwritten manuscript is preserved in his papers, and there is no record of an earlier publication.

11. Kent Larson raises the possibility of a novella or narrative poem published in 1840 or 1841 by the Mormon Nauvoo resident Lyman Omer Littlefield. In 1841, Littlefield published a poem entitled *The Latter Day Saints* under the name "Omer, author of *Eliza, or, the Broken Vow.*" This earlier work is presumed to have been published in the *Illinois Republican* before 1841, but no copies have ever been found, and we can only make guesses about its genre. See Kent Larson's "Desperately

Nonetheless, *The Mormoness, or, The Trials of Mary Maverick* is an extremely important text in the development of Mormonism in literature in the nineteenth century—much more important than Marrayat's novel, which does little more than plagiarize descriptions of Nauvoo from John C. Bennett's *History of the Saints, or, An Expose of Joe Smith and Mormonism*, which was published the year before. Russell's novella, on the other hand, is a wholly original creation by a writer deeply invested in the people and places he describes.

The genesis of *The Mormoness* lies in the story of Philinda Merrick, whose husband and son were killed in the Haun's Mill Massacre of October 30, 1838. In that bloody episode of the so-called Missouri Mormon War, a militia unit from Livingston County, Missouri, attacked a Mormon settlement in Caldwell County, Missouri, killing seventeen Mormon men and young boys. The Merricks were not residents of that community, but were traveling and only coincidentally happened to be at Haun's Mill during the attack. It does not appear that Russell conducted any more research into the life of Philinda Merrick.[12] He took what he knew and imagined the circumstances of her conversion and the life she chose after her family had been taken from her by the mob. Though the narrator refers to the Mormons as a "deluded sect," the book has little to do with doctrines or theologies. It is a book about Mormon identity, and it is built on the same two arguments that Russell made to the *Warsaw Signal* fifteen years earlier: first, the persecution of the Mormons constituted a "meditated outrage upon the rights of native born

---

(or not) Seeking Eliza" at *A Motley Vision*, October 13, 2011, http://www.motleyvision.org/2011/desperately-or-not-seeking-eliza/.

12. In his reminiscences of his father, Spencer G. Russell writes incorrectly that Merrick's wife "came back to Illinois to her friends, and not to Nauvoo, for she was not herself a very bigoted Mormon" (Spencer G. Russell, 106). Philinda Merrick did go on to Nauvoo and join with the Saints after Haun's Mill. That this fact was not recorded in Russell family lore suggests that John did not attempt to trace the life of the woman who served as the model for his heroine.

American citizens"; and second, that "persecution and bloodshed have always increased the persecuted sect."[13] These two threads come together in the most powerful and affecting scene in the story: the murder of Mary's son Eddy—a horrific act of persecution that set Mary's identity forever as "The Mormoness":

> Eddy, even in this fearful hour, disdaining all supplications for his life, proudly drew up his form to its utmost height, and said, *"I am an American!"* Poor, mistaken, deluded child—he had read the history of his country, and vainly supposed that the very name of *"American"* would throw around his rights a shield of adamant. But the proud claim of the boy, and the wild pleadings of the young mother, were alike disregarded. Vorne replied, with a coarse, fiendish laugh, *"kill the young wolves, and there will be no old ones!"* Saying this, he coolly and deliberately brought his rifle within a foot of the child's head, and blew out his brains, sprinkling the clothes of the mother with the blood of her own child.[14]

From this point on, Mary Maverick's life tests the question of whether or not a person who identifies as a Mormon can also be considered a Christian. The answer is yes. Mary becomes someone who devotes herself "to the single purpose of doing good to others."[15] In true Christian fashion, Mary's compassion and desire to serve pushes her further and further outward to the margins of her society. She cares for a dying Roman Catholic girl and ministers to her spiritual needs without judging her religious beliefs. She then moves into a Shawnee Indian village and starts a school for girls. And when a cholera epidemic breaks out among the Indians, Mary becomes a healer—at great risk to her own life. "Death, in the frightful form of cholera, might await her," the narrator muses, "but, whether life or death was to be her lot, she felt that the path of duty was always the path of safety, and the only one."[16]

---

13. *The Mormoness*, 38, 69, 57. Page numbers are for original pagination (enclosed in brackets{} in text.)

14. Ibid., 70.

15. Ibid., 77.

16. Ibid., 78.

By the end of Mary Maverick's story, two facts are indisputable. First, the heroine is entirely Mormon. She is not merely "a Mormon" or "a Mormoness." She is "THE MORMONESS"—a woman whose identity is entirely contained in a statement of her religious affiliation, which has been sanctified by the blood of her only child. At the same time, she is fully Christian. She has devoted her life to the care of others, with no regard for their economic situation or social position. And when confronted with her greatest enemy—the man who murdered her husband and son and deprived her of everything in her life that mattered—she offers him not only compassion, but also forgiveness.

The portrayal of a Mormon character as an indisputable type of Christ was a truly remarkable thing at a time when nearly everything written about Mormons was either pro-Mormon propaganda or anti-Mormon invective. Russell wrote in the same decade that produced such patently anti-Mormon novels as Robert Richards's *The Californian Crusoe* (1854) and Alfreda Bell's *Boadicea the Mormon Wife* (1855). *The Mormoness* is a balanced narrative that does not overpraise the Latter-day Saints nor accept their theology but, at the same time, does acknowledge both their right to exist and their capacity for goodness. It would take another fifty years—and the publication of Lily Dougal's *The Mormon Prophet* (1899)—for an American writer to publish a similarly balanced account of the Mormon experience.

Some Notes on the Text and Appendices

The Mormoness was first published as a serial in the *Alton Courier* between August 5 and September 9 of 1853. The book's five chapters were distributed across six weekly installments printed each Friday. Soon thereafter, it was published by the Courier Steam Press as the second half of the book, *Claudine Lavalle, or, the First Convict; [and] The Mormoness, or, The Trials of Mary Maverick*. Page numbers from the original text have been included in brackets { } for those wishing to cite the original edition, in which the Mormoness begins on page 37. The text has been transcribed as it was originally typeset, with the original punctuation, spelling, and capitalization preserved. In a handful of cases, letters missing from the original typesetting have been supplied in square brackets: admir[a]tion.

In order to provide context for the story, three appendices have been included. The first of these, Spencer G. Russell's 1901 article on his father for the Illinois State Historical Society, gives a good outline of Russell's life and explains the circumstances that led to the writing of *The Mormoness*. This is one of the most important sources that we have for understanding Russell's life and the context for his writings.

The second appendix contains the full text of Russell's 1841 letter to Thomas Gregg defending the Nauvoo Mormons and criticizing the *Warsaw Signal* for its stridently anti-Mormon editorial policy. In this letter we see Russell drawing a very clear distinction between theological disagreement and persecution, arguing that the *Signal's* editorial policy would incite riots against the Mormons in Western Illinois and, in the process, deprive Joseph Smith and his followers of their right as American citizens to exercise their religion as they saw fit. He also predicted, quite correctly, that these persecutions would destroy the Mormon settlement in Nauvoo but would only make the Church stronger in the long run.

The third appendix comes from Russell's 1846 book *The Serpent Uncoiled: A Full-Length Picture of Universalism*. In this selection we see Russell the Baptist preacher engaging with another religion that he sees as incorrect and dangerous to the spiritual life of his community. We include it here to show the contrast between his balanced view of Mormonism and his almost entirely negative view of Universalism. Among other things, it shows that Russell was capable of much harsher criticisms than those he leveled at the Mormons in *The Mormoness, or, The Trials of Mary Maverick.*

Timeline for John Russell

1793: Born July 31 in Cavendish, Windsor County, Vermont.

1807: Apprenticed to Preston Merrifield, a bookbinder in Windsor, Vermont.

1812: At the age of 19, writes his first book, *The Authentic History of the Vermont State's Prison*, on a commission from the state clerk.

1814: Enters Middlebury College in Middlebury, Vermont.

1817: Joins the Baptist Church while teaching in Vergennes, Vermont; meets Laura Ann Spencer and becomes engaged; graduates from Middlebury and marries Laura in Whitewater, Indiana, while traveling west with his family.

1819: Moves to the St. Louis area to become a tutor; sometime between 1819 and 1821, he writes a brief essay called "The Venomous Worm," which is incorporated into the Fourth Grade *McGuffey Reader*.

1828: Moves to a farm in Illinois in an area that he names Bluffdale; teaches at several high schools in the vicinity. He maintains this residence throughout his life, though he has several periods of extended work-related absence.

1829: Appointed Postmaster of Bluffdale, a position that he holds for the rest of his life and passes on to his son when he dies.

1833: Licensed as a Baptist minister; begins teaching at the Alton Academy in Alton, Illinois, a school founded by fellow Baptist minister John Mason Peck.

1833: Writes "The Spectre Hunter," the first of several pieces of short fiction that he publishes in the *Western Monthly Magazine*.

1833–1834: Parley P. Pratt, William McLellin, and other well-known Mormons meet with Russell and his wife during their missionary travels in Illinois and are received warmly.

1836: Begins regular correspondence with Thomas Gregg, influential Illinois journalist who will later edit the *Warsaw Signal*.

1837: Becomes the founding editor of the *Backwoodsman*, a periodical based in Grafton, Illinois, devoted to "foreign and domestic intelligence, literature, agriculture, and the news of the day." Edits the paper until 1839.

1838: Hosts Sidney Rigdon and Parley P. Pratt in his home, after the Mormons have been driven out of Missouri, and hears the story of Philinda Merrick, whose husband and son were killed at Haun's Mill. This story will become the basis of *The Mormoness*.

1841: Writes a July 7 letter to Thomas Gregg criticizing the *Warsaw Signal* for its harsh anti-Mormon editorial policy. When Gregg takes over the *Signal* from Thomas Sharp in 1842, he significantly moderates the paper's anti-Mormonism.

1841–1842: Moves temporarily to Louisville, Kentucky, to edit the *Louisville Advertiser*.

1843–1849: Moves temporarily to Clinton, Louisiana, where he is the principal of Spring Hill Academy and the Superintendent of public schools.

1849–1850: Teaches high school in Carrolton, Illinois.

1850: Retires from teaching and devotes himself exclusively to his writing.

1853: Publishes *The Mormoness, or, The Trials of Mary Maverick* as a serial in the *Alton Courier* between August 5 and September 9.

1854: *Claudine Lavalle, or, The First Convict* and *The Mormoness, or, The Trials of Mary Maverick* published as a single book by the Courier Steam Press.

1862: Awarded an honorary doctoral degree from the University of Chicago.

1863: Dies on January 21 at sixty-nine years old at his home in Bluffdale, Illinois.

Bibliography of John Russell's Works

Alice Wade and *Lame Isaac*. New York: Sheldon, Blakeman and Company, 1859.

The Authentic History of the Vermont State's Prison. Wright and Sibley Printers, 1812.

"Bluffdale." *Illinois Monthly Magazine* 2 (February 1832): 207–11.

Claudine Lavalle, or, The First Convict and *The Mormoness, or, The Trials of Mary Maverick*. Alton [Ill.]: Courier Steam Press, 1853.

"The Emigrant." *Western Monthly Magazine, and Literary Journal* 3 (1835): 67–82.

"Flora Jarvis; or, The Young Wife's Plea for the Maine Law." *Alton Weekly Courier*, July 6, 1854.

"A Glimpse at the Future, Three Hundred Years Hence—a Prophecy." *Illinois Monthly Magazine* (November 1830); reprint, *Publication of the Illinois State Historical Society* 9 (1904): 435–40.

Going to Mill. Philadelphia: American Baptist Publication Society, 1858.

Little Granite, or, The New Hampshire Boy. New York: Sheldon, Blakeman and Company, 1859.

"The Mormoness, or, The Trials of Mary Maverick, a Narrative of Real Events." *Alton Weekly Courier*, July–August 1853.

"The Piasa: An Indian Tradition of Illinois," *Alton Evening Telegraph*, September 28, 1836.

[A Western Layman, pseud.] *The Serpent Uncoiled: A Full-Length Picture of Universalism*. American Baptist Publication Society, 1846.

"The Specter Hunter, A Legend of the West." *Western Monthly Magazine, and Literary Journal* 1 (1833): 458–66.

"Sir William Dean, or, The Magic of Wealth." *Western Monthly Magazine, and Literary Journal* 2 (1834): 37–46.

"The Venomous Worm." *St. Charles Missourian* in 1819 or 1821. Reprinted in William William, *The Eclectic Fourth Reader: Containing Elegant Extracts in Prose and Poetry from the Best American and English Writers.* Cincinnati: Truman and Smith, 1838, and in multiple later editions.

THE MORMONESS;

OR, THE

TRIALS OF MARY MAVERICK

A NARRATIVE OF REAL EVENTS

by

John Russell

1853

CHAPTER I.

"Delusion! Ah! The *weak* may be deluded,
But is the learned, the enlightened, noble Varus,
The victim of delusion?—It cannot be!
I'll not believe it."—*The Martyr*[1]

{37} *Halloo! Halloo!* uttered in the loudest tones of the human voice, instantly brought the little family of James Maverick to the door. At the gate was the well-known son of a neighbor, mounted upon a shaggy, half-broken colt, which he was fond of riding because it was his own. The animal seemed resolved, by his rearing and pitching, of which the boy was not a little proud, to give his rider no opportunity of performing his errand. But, at length, with many interruptions, intermingled with the frequent cry of "who-a! who-a, Tecumseh," the message was delivered, and the youth and his steed were on their way to the next neighbor's to deliver there the same tidings.

That young man was the son of Deacon Hezekiah Cobb, a worthy old farmer of that settlement, whose house was known far and near to the religious community by the expressive name of "*Pilgrim's Tavern*." Not only preachers of the gospel, but professors of religion of every stripe, found a welcome under his hospitable roof. The very sight of his well-filled barn often made the veriest "*backslider*" devout. Many and many a church member, seldom suspected, at home, of being righteous overmuch, has driven his weary horses ten miles beyond a tavern to put up for the night with the good deacon, rather than stay with "the people of the world."

He had sent his son to acquaint the inhabitants of the settlement, far and near, that a Mormon had arrived at his house, and would preach in the school-house that night, at early candle light.

---

1. *The Martyr* is an 1826 poetic drama by the Scottish poet and playwright Joanna Baillie (1762–1851).

{38} This intelligence excited the most intense interest all over the populous settlement of Sixteen Mile Prairie, for the Mormons were then comparatively few in number, and nothing known of them in that region, except from report. Rumor indeed with her hundred tongues, had informed the public that Joe Smith, the founder of the sect, was regarded by his infatuated followers as a prophet—that he pretended to have dug up a set of Golden Plates inscribed with Hebrew characters, which, by miraculous agency, he had translated—that these writings were received by them as a Revelation, and were printed as such under the name of the *"Book of Mormon."* It was likewise known that these self-styled *"Latter-Day Saints"* claimed the power of healing the sick, and of working various other miracles. A thousand reports were in circulation, that exhibited both their doctrines and practices in a very unfavorable light, and these rumors, however absurd or contradictory, gained implicit belief. It was a subject of wonder that any human being of sane mind could be deluded into a belief in Mormonism.

The secret enemies of the Christian religion, whom a regard for their own reputation restrained from uttering their sentiments openly against divine revelation, were loud against the Mormons. In assailing their claims to working miracles and other professions, they leveled many a blow, safely, that bore equally hard upon the miracles of the Scriptures. Among the truly pious, Mormonism was regarded with sorrow, not unmingled with indignation against its leaders.

Such was the state of public opinion at that period upon the subject of the new sect, generally. In Sixteen Mile Prairie there could probably have been found one, in the whole length and breadth of the settlement, who would not have resented, as a gross insult, the bare suggestion that he might one day become a friend to the Mormons.

Even at this early period in their history, the Latter-Day Saints were met at every point with a most deadly hostility. Hundreds who had lived godless lives suddenly felt so much zeal for pure and undefiled religion, that they could not endure the false doctrines of the Mormons, and would gladly have exterminated the whole sect.

Among all the enemies of this deluded sect, there could hardly have been found one more determined, more unrelenting in his opposition, than James Maverick. He was an intelligent, well-informed man, and had read, with eager interest, every thing upon the subject with which the newspapers of his day teemed. With the history of the sect he was familiar, and had pondered upon every incident of it, from the discovery of the Golden Plates down to the last feature which this ever-varying delusion had assumed. {39}

No phrenologist accustomed to the study of human character would have doubted, for a moment, that the feelings of young Maverick would be deeply excited upon every subject that enlisted his attention. His high, broad forehead and prominently developed mental organs displayed, in no ordinary degree, firmness of mind, reverence and conscientiousness, traits of character so conspicuous in the early martyrs. His large blue eyes, fringed with long and drooping eye-lashes, gave to his countenance, especially when he was buried in silent thought, a faint shade of melancholy.

And yet, these manly and even stern traits of character were not unmingled with milder developments. The veriest stranger would have read in his frank, open countenance, kindness of heart and disinterested benevolence.

Almost from childhood, like his wife, he had been a church member, and his deportment through all that period attested the sincerity of his profession. Even the most unblushing scoffer paid an involuntary tribute to James Maverick. Judge Maverick, his father, who belonged to the same denomination, had held many important offices in one of the Eastern States, where, by industry and economy, he had acquired a competency. A few years previous to the opening of this story, Judge Maverick had removed to Greene country, Illinois and purchased a large tract of land in Sixteen Mile Prairie. He gave to James, his eldest and only married son, a quarter section, distant some three miles from his own residence, erected for him a neat dwelling house, enabled him to place a part of his farm under cultivation, and supplied him liberally with stock. Active, enterprising and intelligent, aided heart and hand by his little wife, whom he devotedly loved, their farm and every thing around them soon assumed an air of successful industry and rural happiness, that often drew from the passing traveler involuntary expressions of admiration. An old neighbor of theirs frequently declared that the sun actually shone brighter upon the farm, and especially around the dwelling of James and Mary Maverick, than it did anywhere else in the whole settlement. It is quite possible that the old man, had he been a chemist skilled in the analysis of kindly affection, would have discovered that much of the sunshine around the cottage of the Mavericks was merely the sunshine of their own hearts.

Be that as it may, it must nevertheless be confessed that no object seen in all the wide landscape of Sixteen Mile was more pleasing to the eye than that simple cottage. All along its sides the scarlet trumpet {40} flower, the Bignonia and the Lonicera, had been trained by Mary to climb to the very eaves. In early summer, when the broad, bell-shaped blossoms hung in festoons along the walls, and over the windows, troops of humming birds were seen, from early dawn till sunset, darting from flower to flower. The busy, pattering feet of "Little Eddy" stood still in speechless admiration, as he watched the hummingbirds as they hung quivering in air over the blossom for a moment, and then darted away, swift as a ray of light, to sip the honey from some other flower. He gazed with absorbed attention upon the bright-winged butter-flies, and the wild bees that hovered around, drinking the fragrance of the flowers. At such times the young mother, almost as childlike as little Eddy himself, would often watch with absorbing interest the varying expression of his features, without uttering a word, or daring to stir, so fearful was she of breaking the spell. Her eyes not unfrequently grew moist as she thus gazed upon him, and her lips moved, but uttered no sound audible to mortal ears.

The brief snatches of time which more serious duties did not claim were usually devoted by her to ornamenting their home, that she might render it more attractive to her husband and child. With a broad sun-bonnet upon her head, and little Eddy at her side, as a special reward to him for being good, she tended the flowers and shrubs she had planted in the yard. Rare plants, that required but little care beyond daily watering, ornamented her windows in summer, and in the cold, leaf-less season of winter afforded an air of cheerfulness to the parlor. Aside from her own love of the beautiful, she had still another object. She was desirous that her child, with the earliest dawn of a wakening mind, should acquire a love for the cheap pleasures which nature has poured out with so liberal a hand to all who know the value of her rich treasures. She believed that the youth who can derive enjoyment from the beautiful and the sublime of nature, whether seen in the rushing torrent, the towering cliff, the rifted storm-cloud, the lofty oak whose broad top had bid defiance to the tempests of many a century, the wide sweep of a western prairie, or the humble flower, had acquired not only a source of unfailing enjoyment, but also no mean safe-guard of virtue. She wished to render all the early and most hallowed recollections of his childhood, in after years, endearing memories of his mother and his home.

We trust that our readers, should we be so fortunate as to have any, will pardon us for dwelling thus long and minutely upon the character of Mary Maverick, for we are describing a real personage, and not an {41} imaginary being. At the risk of being tedious, we shall attempt to lay her character open to the reader, that he may know fully the heart of the little woman who is doomed to meet the buffeting of the storm.

Let it not be imagined that Sixteen Mile Prairie so nearly resembled paradise, that the ambition of Mary Maverick to render her home attractive excited no envy, malice, or ill-will. To some of her neighbors, and especially of her own sex, the shrubbery and flowers of the little woman were really gall and wormwood. Unkind remarks upon the subject were not unfrequently made to Mary herself, but more frequently they reached her ear through the officious zeal of some visitor, who professed to be the defender of the abused little woman. These reports produced

but a slight and momentary impression upon the mind of Mrs.
Maverick, who listened to them with a smile, and not unfrequently, when anything more than usually spiteful was uttered,
burst into a merry laugh, and in ten minutes forgot all about it.
It was far otherwise with her husband. He felt these carpings of
envy and malice more deeply than he was willing to confess; and
it sometimes required all her soothing influence, which she knew
well how to exert, to induce him to refrain from openly expressing his resentment to her detractors. One evening a neighboring
lady called upon them, at a time when Mrs. Maverick chanced
to be watering a large and beautiful moss rose, whose numerous
blossoms filled the whole room with their fragrance. "Is not that
beautiful, Mrs. Jones?" exclaimed the delighted husband to their
visitor, pointing to the rose. The walk of that lady through the
yard, between rows of shrubs and flowers, had already excited her
ill-humor, which instantly broke forth at the remark of the gratified husband. "Oh, yes," she exclaimed, "beautiful, no doubt;
but anybody can have just such, if they choose. I could plant
shrubbery just as well as your wife, Mr. Maverick, but I have
something else to do. Mary finds time every day to read, teach
her boy, tend flowers, and paint these pictures that hang up here
on the wall; but while she is doing this, I am making butter and
cheese, using my needle, or attending to my work." This broad
and undisguised insinuation that Mary neglected her household
duties for these amusements, was rather more than the patience
of her husband could bear. It was the drop too much that made
the cup overflow. Maverick instantly sprang from his seat, and,
in spite of the look of entreaty from his wife, bowing with mock
deference and humility to Mrs. Jones, begged her to accompany
him and Mary. He led their visitor into their little dairy, where
everything was perfectly neat and in order, and showed Mrs.
Jones the rows of rich {42} cheese that adorned the shelves. He
then conducted her to the cellar, where, in a cool place, jars of
butter were packed, yellow as gold.

On their return to the parlor, Maverick remarked: "I do not
know how much sewing you have done this year, Mrs. Jones,

but Mary has not only done our own, but paid, with her needle, for all the groceries we have used." The neighbor, who could find no time to read, teach a child, or water a flower, confessed that Mary in addition to all these, had accomplished much more than she had done, and more than she would have believed it possible for any woman to do. "I will tell you the secret of all that, Mrs. Jones, if you will be quite sure not to repeat it to any one." Then leaning his head toward the lady, as if about to reveal an important secret, Maverick whispered, "the truth is, Mrs. Jones, that Mary is a *witch*."

We have already informed our readers that Maverick was deadly hostile to the Mormons. Not that he would persecute or invade the rights of any sect, but was violently opposed to giving them any encouragement whatever. Joe Smith he could never hear named without uttering an expression of deep indignation. The newspapers informed him that converts were making by scores, and that, too, from orthodox churches. Men whom he had known from childhood at the East—had known at the vanguard of the sacramental host, had fallen into the fatal snare of Joe Smith, sold their possessions, accumulated by a life of toil and privations, and taken up their lot with the Latter-Day Saints.

Mrs. Maverick, though decidedly opposed to the progress of Mormonism, by no means shared in the vindictive feelings of her husband against that sect. There was too much of gentleness and goodness in her heart to find room for such emotions, even against the vilest of the human race. She had often tried to soften the asperity of her husband's feelings toward the Mormons, but in vain.

The intelligence that a Mormon preacher had actually come to that settlement, to propagate their pernicious doctrines among the inhabitants of Sixteen Mile Prairie, was utterly astounding. It came as unexpectedly and unlooked for as a clap of thunder in a cloudless day, or an earthquake which no previous token had announced. We shall not attempt to describe the indignation with which Maverick heard this unwelcome news. "Can anything be done to prevent this calamity, now that it has come to our very doors?" was his first inquiry, made in his own mind. He had the power, as one of the School Directors, to forbid the use of the school house to the Mormon preacher. But that course was repugnant to his feelings, as a violation of the principles of {43} religious toleration. Besides, if thus denied the use of the school house, public sympathy would instantly be awakened in behalf of the preacher, and a dozen houses at once be thrown open to him, giving to Mormonism a ten-fold greater influence than it would otherwise have. The sun was hardly an hour high, and he had no time to go over the settlement and try to persuade the people not to attend the preaching, even if such a course promised success. At any rate, he could insure the absence of one family. His seat and that of his wife should be vacant, and thus set a silent, but most impressive seal upon the attendance of all who were present—a condemnation which would have a decided influence against Mormonism. Such was his resolve, in the absence of all other means of warding off the threatened calamity.

Few, perhaps, would have anticipated any opposition to this arrangement from the gentle Mary. But oppose it she did. She had felt no desire to attend the meeting; but the moment her husband, in an arbitrary manner, resolved, without consulting her at all, that she should stay at home, an ardent desire to hear the Mormon took possession of her heart. She attempted to reason him out of his exclusion, but in vain. Though yielding as the sensitive plant at the voice of kindness, the little woman could be firm and immovable as the Rock of Gibraltar, when her rights were disregarded, and her feelings touched by a rude hand. On such an occasion an instantaneous change came over her whole being. She uttered no complaints, no reproaches, but her whole soul seemed to retire within itself.

We cannot determine what course either of them would have pursued, or which yielded, for just at this moment a new actor in the scene entered, and changed the entire current of passing events.

This was no other than Frank Maverick, the youngest and favorite brother, a warm-hearted, intelligent youth of seventeen, who carried sunshine with him wherever he went, and was every where a welcome guest.

Filled with excitement at the novelty of hearing a follower of Joe Smith, and elated with the anticipation of seeing a crowd of people at the meeting, he cried out before he crossed his brother's threshhold, "get ready, Sister Mary; get ready to go and hear a sermon out of the Golden Plates; and be sure that you put on your best bib and tucker, and what is better yet, your brightest smiles—mind, your *very* brightest smiles—for you are going to have a beau wait upon you to-night that *is* a beau, and not an old fellow twenty-six years old, like brother James there. Mother, who always thinks of everything and always just at the {44} right time, said she knew that your husband could not be coaxed to lay down his hatred of Mormonism long enough to hear one preach, and so she sent your very humble servant, Mr. Francis Marion Maverick, usually named, for the sake of brevity, *Frank*, so that your ladyship should have no excuse for staying at home, when she and everybody else and everybody else's wife and children are all sure to be there. But, sister Mary," said the young man, gazing around with admiration, "how beautiful your flowers have grown. If ever I look out for a wife, I mean to try to find one just like you, and the very first question I intend to ask her is, whether she is fond of flowers." "Ah, brother Frank!" replied Mary with an arch smile, "I half suspect that you have just come from taking a lesson on flowers from pretty Lucy Mills, and that she gave you the rose you wear so jauntily in the button-hole of your vest, just over your heart." The young man blushed deeply at his shrewd guess of sister Mary, but laughed aloud, and, to conceal his consciousness that she had hit the very truth, he seized little Eddy, who had run in from the garden at the welcome sound of "Uncle Frank's" voice, and swinging the child over his shoulder, trotted out of the house with Eddy upon his back.

CHAPTER II.

And must I leave thee?—leave those loving eyes,
　Whose beams to me are like the sun to flowers,
The only joys that in my bosom rise,
　Bidding to bloom upon life's desert hours?
Leave thee, and wander to some desert shore,
Where thy young form can glad my eyes no more?"
Joanna Baillie[1]

We have given the reader a short chapter, that he might pause for a moment over the scenes we have depicted, before he proceeded to others of more thrilling interest. We will now proceed, gentle reader.

It was speedily settled that Frank, who would stay all night at the house of his brother, should attend Mary to the meeting. James still persevered in his obstinate determination to remain at home with little Eddy. This arrangement instantly brought a cloud over the sunny features of the child, who would thus lose the opportunity of going with his mother and uncle Frank. But his father turned all these sorrows into joy by promising to show him the moon and stars in the magic lantern. "Oh yes," cried the now delighted boy, clapping his hands in {45} high glee, "Oh yes, father, and the Mexican mouse trap, too?" "Yes, Eddy, and the Mexican mouse trap, too," was the reply.

Night came, and Frank Maverick, proud of sister Mary, and always happy to be her attendant, departed, with the little woman upon his arm. Hardly had the sound of the gate closing behind them reached the ears of the impatient Eddy, when he claimed the performance of his father's promise to show him the moon, stars, and the Mexican mouse trap.

---

1. No poem with these lines appears in the 1853 edition of *The Dramatic and Poetical Works of Joanna Baillie*. The poem is included in an article entitled "The Sports of Ammon" that appeared in *The American Monthly* 2 (1836): 81. The author, "H," has been identified as Charles Fenno Hoffman (*The New Yorker*, July 16, 1836, 202).

Some months previously, a young man came to the settlement to deliver a course of astronomical lectures. Among other apparatus, he had a magic lantern, by means of which he exhibited to the audience a magnified view of a map of the moon, and various phenomena of the heavenly bodies. At the close of each lecture he amused the juvenile portion of his audience by exhibiting to them several ludicrous pictures, and among the rest, one which he facetiously called "the Mexican mouse trap," which convulsed the whole audience with laughter.

This young man was taken sick, and for a long time his life was despaired of. During the long period of his illness, he was at the house of young Maverick, and received from him and Mary every attention in the power of kindness to bestow. When he became convalescent, and was about to depart, the family would receive no compensation for the time and expense which they had so freely bestowed, Mr. Maverick drily remarking to the invalid, that it was quite enough for him to suffer the pain of sickness, without having to pay for it.

Having resolved to abandon lecturing and engage in other pursuits, and knowing how pleased little Eddy had been with the pictures of the magic lantern, he presented that instrument and the accompanying drawings to the child, as a testimonial of gratitude to the parents which he knew would be doubly acceptable when bestowed upon their child.

On the night of the Mormon preaching, Mr. Maverick, with Eddy for his sole audience, exhibited all the views in the collection of the late lecturer. When he threw the ma[gn]ified image of the moon, the other planets and the fixed stars, in succession, upon the white wall of the darkened room, he explained to the child, in simple and familiar language, the immense size and distance of the heavenly bodies. As little Eddy listened to his father, the shade of new and deep thoughts came over his expressive features, and leaning his head upon his hands, he sat for some moments silent and absorbed, as if attempting to comprehend the wonders that his father had been unfolding. But Eddy was a child, and it was natural that he should prefer pictures of a less {46} serious cast. In this wish he was fully gratified, and the evening was one of rare enjoyment to the happy child. After having laughed and clapped his little hands at the tenth exhibition which the indulgent father gave him of the Mexican mouse trap, he became tired, even of pleasure and not a little sleepy. After listening to the accustomed evening prayer of his child, Mr. Maverick put him to bed, and immediately Eddy was fast asleep.

Everything in and around the house was now wrapped in silence and repose. Not a sound was heard but the ticking of a high, old-fashioned clock, as its long pendulum swung from side to side, marking with its measured sweep the flight of time. It was an hour well calculated to call forth the memory of the past, and awaken the hallowed emotions of the soul. He thought of his absent wife. Everything in the room bore the impress of her industry and affection. What did he not owe to the gentle being who had made his home so happy? With her affection, he could bid defiance to adversity. But had he always repaid her devotedness with the gentleness so richly merited? His own acts and bearing toward her passed in review before his mind, and he resolved that if in any instance he had been harsh or unkind in word or look, he would be more just to her in future.

The cheerful voices of his wife and Frank, just returned in high glee from the meeting, were now heard. The crowd of people present, the novelty of the occasion and the pleasure of an evening walk, all tended to enliven their spirits. "Well, Mary, I am glad to see you back again," was the salutation of the husband, in the most kind and cheerful tones of his voice. "How many people were there?—a house full, I dare say. And what had the old fellow to say for himself?" At the latter inquiry both Frank and Mary burst into a hearty laugh. "Old fellow," said she, "why! he is not a year older than twenty-six, if he is even so old as that, and he is quite polished in his manners, too, and does not look at all as I expected a Mormon would. But, dear me, I forgot that you will see him for yourself to-morrow, for he is going to call here in the morning. Mrs. Cobb, where he is staying, introduced him after the services were over, to most of the ladies present, and when he heard my name, he said he was acquainted with you some years ago, and would be glad to see you again. So I could do no less than invite him to come here, though I knew you would rather he would be in Jericho than call upon you." "You did right, Mary, as you always do. I should have been sorry had my wife been so wanting in hospitality, or rather in common civility, as not to invite even a Mormon under *such* circumstances." {47}

While this conversation was going on, Mary had taken off her bonnet and shawl; then stepping lightly to the bed-side of little Eddy, and gazing for a moment upon the bright vision of her child in the sweet and peaceful sleep of innocence, she stooped down and imprinted a warm kiss upon his forehead. The child did not awake, but it seemed as if even in sleep he knew the fond kiss of his mother's lips, for at their light touch a happy smile played over his features.

Neither Mary nor Frank could recollect the preacher's name, as it was so uncommon. Maverick, after puzzling his brain for a long time to no purpose, in conjecturing who among all his former acquaintances the Mormon preacher could possibly be, abandoned the attempt as hopeless. "But what did he preach about? What did he say? Did he take his text from the Book of Mormon?" were the inquiries he addressed to his young brother. "The text?" replied Frank, with much embarrassment, "the text? Really, I disremember all about it. Ah! I recollect now. He had Deacon Cobb's big bible, and read his text from about the middle of it, so all was right of course." "Well, well, Frank," replied his brother with a loud laugh, not a little amused at his utter inattention to the sermon, "you are remarkably intelligent." "Oh, you must not expect brother Frank, or any one else," replied Mary, "to be intelligent, as you call it, upon every subject. If you were to question him upon some other subject, Lucy Mills' bonnet, for instance, I do assure you he could tell you all about it, for I saw his eyes in that direction, even in the most eloquent part of the sermon." A laugh followed, in which Frank joined as heartily as the others. But when her husband questioned her about the text, and the subject of the discourse, Mary was found to have been quite as inattentive as Frank, and the laugh now turned upon her.

The family soon after retired to rest, and all was still. But James Maverick found it impossible for him to sleep. His thoughts were too busy for repose. He could not banish the Mormons from his mind. He reasoned with himself that the visit of the preacher on the occasion was an affair of no consequence whatever, and yet his mind was disturbed on that point. Nothing, indeed, could be easier than for him to refute every argument that could be produced in favor of Mormonism. A child could expose the fraud of the Golden Plates, the very foundation upon which all their doctrines rested. Perhaps divine Providence had so ordered it, that the visit of the preacher to him was designed as the means by which his mind was to be freed from the snare that Joe Smith had woven around him. Good to the young man was evidently {48} the design. Why then should it thus disturb him? He would drive it from his thoughts, and address himself to sleep. But all these efforts were in vain. Sleep would not visit his pillow. Hours at length went by since the family retired to rest, and it was long past midnight. He could hear the low, soft breathing of his wife, and the still gentler sound of his child, and again did he resolutely attempt to divert his mind from the theme that so harrassed and disturbed him. Casually turning his eye toward the window, a single bright star was visible through the folds of the curtain. He would bend all his thoughts upon that star, for any theme was better than Mormonism. In a moment more a cloud veiled the star, and shut it out from his vision. At last, sleep, so long and earnestly sought, visited his pillow, but his slumber was disturbed by frightful dreams. He seemed in his sleep to hear low, mournful sounds, that came sighing upon the night air, and seemed borne from a great distance. Their tone was soft and melancholy as the dirge which the Angel of the covenant is supposed by some to wail over a lost soul.

Could this be a presentiment of approaching evil, a warning sent him from the invisible world that woes were at hand? We can know but little either of the power of disembodied spirits, or their agency in the affairs of mortals. We do know, however, that the globe we inhabit, and the myriads of worlds posted like sentinels on the confines of infinite space, were made, and all their motions yet are governed by an invisible spirit. Revelation teaches us that hosts of invisible spirits take a deep interest in our happiness, while hosts of fallen angels ever employ their wiles to lure mankind to ruin. May it not be true, then, as the early Fathers of the church believed and taught, that a Guardian Angel hovers, unseen, around the good and the true, standing nightly at their pillows, and giving them mysterious intimations of the near approach of trials, danger and woe? But we have penetrated already too far, perhaps, into the dimly lighted regions of conjecture, and will now resume the narration of passing events.

The morning came, and, contrary to his usual custom of rising with the dawn, Mr. Maverick still slept. His wife, suspecting that he had passed a restless night, not only avoided waking him, but delayed her breakfast beyond the usual hour, and called him only when she could delay no longer, without fear of their expected visitor finding him in bed. He arose, a shade paler than usual, but with his accustomed flow of spirits. The day was one of the loveliest that spring puts forth in this genial climate. The sun was pouring a flood of light upon the {49} verdant prairie. The air was soft and bland. Not a cloud stained the deep blue vault of heaven. The mocking birds, whose nests were in the trees and shrubbery of the yard, were pouring forth many a mild trill, and imitating in turn the song of every bird of the forest, field, or grove.

The feelings of Maverick were in unison with the scenery around him. The dark, deep, mysterious forebodings of the previous night had all vanished. His long hours of sleepless excitement were remembered with astonishment and mortification at his own weakness of mind. The approaching visit of the Mormon was now regarded in its true light, as an affair, indeed, of no earthly consequence, one way or the other—a very trifling, unimportant event. He could hardly believe it possible that he could have given it a moment's attention.

After breakfast, Mr. Maverick occupied himself with labors in sight of the house, in momentary expectation of the arrival of the preacher. Hour after hour rolled by, and noon came, but no visitor. He had promised to call early in the morning, and they now concluded that he had abandoned the intention of visiting them, and gone some five miles distant on the road to-wards Alton to the place at which he had appointed to preach that night. They were congratulating themselves, soon after dinner, that they had fortunately escaped an interview so un-welcome, when suddenly and unexpectedly a stranger entered the open door. For an instant Maverick gazed upon him with speechless surprise, then, uttering the exclamation, *"Why! Mr. Wilmer!"* sprang from his seat, seized the hand of the stranger, and shook it with the most cordial ratification. He was in the act of introducing the new-comer to his wife, when he learned, to his overwhelming astonishment, that this was no other than the Mormon preacher who had held forth to the people of the settlement the night before, at the school house. Among all his numerous conjectures about the identity of the preacher with any of his old acquaintances, the thought had not once struck him as possible that Mr. Wilmer, of all others, could be deluded into a belief of Mormonism.

Soon after their arrival in Illinois, and their settlement in Sixteen Mile Prairie, James Maverick found it necessary to take a journey of a hundred and twenty miles, to the county seat of one of the counties of this State, lying on the Wabash River. An uncle of his in one of the Eastern States had a claim to a large and valuable tract of land in that region, and employed James to visit the county seat, and, by examining the records of the county, ascertain the validity of his title.

The region through which Maverick had to travel was then thinly {50} inhabited, and portions of his road a mere *"trail,"* indicated only by a foot-path hardly discernible on the prairies, and in the timbered land by here and there a *"blazed tree."*

On arriving at the "Branch" of the Wabash, upon the opposite side of which the town he went to visit was situated, Maverick found that stream, which in the dry season is a mere rill, swollen into a torrent by the long continued and heavy rains. With the utmost difficulty he compelled his high-spirited horse to go onto the bridge. As he did so, Maverick discovered a man standing on the opposite shore, next to the town, who called to him with violent gesticulations. But the loud roar of the booming waters, and the snorting of his frightened horse, prevented him from understanding a word the man uttered.

He had proceeded scarce two-thirds of the distance across, when he perceived that the bridge was in motion. A large floating tree had been hurled with all the force of the current against the end of the bridge he had just passed over, and it was slowly wheeling into the stream. Not an instant must be lost. Life and death hung in equal poise, suspended upon the decision of a moment. He must cross that bridge before the end next to the town had parted from the bank, or be precipitated, horse and rider, into the raging torrent, where nothing that breathed could live a moment. Maverick plunged his spurs up to their rowels into the sides of his horse, which rushed forward as if fully conscious of the peril. The end of the bridge had broken away, and was already several feet from the bank when they arrived. The horse collected all his powers in one mighty effort, and gave a spring. He leaped the yawning chasm and reached the shore. Both were saved. The force and suddenness of the shock threw Maverick with violence to the earth, and the first thing of which he was conscious, he found himself lying in bed in a neatly furnished chamber. The man who had called to him from the shore stood near him, and at his side a gentleman who appeared to be a physician.

Fortunately, Mr. Maverick had broken no bones, nor received any serious injury by his fall. His kind hosts insisted upon his remaining their guest till the high waters had subsided sufficiently to render the bridgeless stream fordable. This hospitable offer was gratefully accepted, and Maverick remained there nearly two weeks, during which he received the kind attentions of that family.

It is needless to repeat that the man whose generous hospitality he had shared was no other than Mr. Wilmer, the individual who now stood before him in the degraded character of a Mormon preacher. What {51} a change had come over that individual, and over all his earthly prospects, since Maverick saw him last! At the period of Maverick's first acquaintance with him, Mr. Wilmer was decidedly the most popular man in that county, held the office of Clerk of the Circuit Court, and other employments that yielded him a large income, and was on the high road to distinction and wealth. And this was the man who preached the night previous, in the settlement of Sixteen Mile Prairie.

The astonishment of Maverick was overwhelming. Could it be possible that Wilmer had been so insane as to fall into the delusion of Joe Smith, and make shipwreck of all his brilliant prospects? He at length made some inquiries about the health of Mrs. Wilmer and their daughter. At the mention of their names, the whole countenance of Wilmer underwent an instantaneous change, and the quiver of his lip betrayed an anguish of mind which he strove in vain to conceal. Mastering his emotions, he calmly replied that his father-in-law had taken them from him soon after he became Mormon; his wife having refused to live with him unless he would renounce that sect, and her father was now pursuing measures to procure for her a divorce. He had made over all his property to his wife and child. "I am now," added he, "literally a homeless wanderer, without a place where to lay my head; but I trust that these light afflictions, which are but for a moment, will work out for me a far more exceeding and eternal weight of glory."

Maverick and his wife listened with deep interest to this relation. Both were affected, but their emotions were widely different. Maverick thought how nobly he would repay the hospitality of that family, by restoring Wilmer again to them, cured of his wild delusion. He doubted not that he could open his eyes to the full absurdity of Mormonism, and he would set about the work with as little delay as possible. Mary, on the contrary, felt no ambition for making proselytes to any creed, but felt in her secret heart that Wilmer's wife was really unworthy of a single regret, and could never have truly loved her husband, or she would have clung to him but the closer, the more the rest of the world cast him off.

The Mormon had appointed to preach that night five miles south of Maverick, and having no means of reaching the place except by walking, Maverick concluded to harness up his horses, and take him there in his wagon. The preacher himself proposed returning with him, and preaching several nights more in that settlement. Unwelcome as this arrangement was to the Mavericks, they felt themselves compelled by a sense of gratitude, and even common civility to their guest, to make no {52} objections. Had it been otherwise, Maverick would have made a decided effort to prevent it.

No attempt was made that afternoon to discuss the doctrines of the Mormon creed, but many preliminary inquiries about the sect, and of their general character, were made. After tea, Maverick and Wilmer set out for the place of meeting. It was dark when they arrived. The candles were already lighted up. A crowd had collected. On the outside of the house, groups of men and full-grown boys were clustered, discussing in a loud tone the subject of the meeting. The rude, coarse jokes uttered against the Mormons were received with boisterous applause.

The preacher passed through the crowd at the door, entered the house, and took his seat at a desk on the opposite side of the room. Giving no heed to the loud whispering and tittering, he commenced by singing a hymn, after which he opened the bible, and read the tenth chapter of Luke. To the disappointment of no small number, who came there for sport, instead of a portion of the Book of Mormon or the Golden Plates, they heard only a deeply impressive chapter from the New Testament. The reading ended, he paused for a moment, then saying, "let us pray," knelt down. There was nothing in the simple act of a minister's kneeling to excite attention, for the practice was common. The whole congregation had been accustomed to that mode from their infancy. But the manner in which that simple act was performed by the Mormon was striking. There was deep humility of soul in every attitude and motion. It seemed as if he wished to prostrate himself in the very dust before Him whom he was about to address. But the prayer, the prayer itself, was still more striking and peculiar. It was uttered in a low, deep tone, but every word was distinctly audible at the remotest corner of the room. He seemed to have forgotten that an audience was around him, prepared to criticise every word he uttered, but appeared to remember only that he was in the presence of the Deity.

Many of the serious portion of the congregation were affected, and even the young men and overgrown boys, who came there for sport, were awed into silence.

He took a text from the Bible, a verse of the same chapter that he had just read. In a sermon of nearly an hour and a half long, he explained the grounds upon which the Latter-Day Saints, the followers of Jo[e] Smith, founded their belief in Mormonism. These doctrines he [d]efended with an ingenuity of argument, and an eloquence that wanted {53} but the simple ingredient of *truth* to render it a model of pulpit oratory.

Unexpectedly to all, he professed to receive the Old and New Testaments as the word of God, and drew from the bible itself all the proofs which he adduced in support of the Mormon creed. Innumerable passages were quoted by him from the bible, which he ingeniously employed to sustain their peculiar doctrines, and the authenticity of the Book of Mormon. They termed themselves "Latter-Day Saints," he said, in reference to the near approach of the "Latter Day," when the Angel, with one foot upon the land and the other on the sea, should declare that time should be no longer. Many striking passages of Scripture were adduced in support of this, and especially from the prophetic books of the Old Testament. The last days of the earth were at their very doors. With ingenious sophistry, various passages which he quoted from the Bible were seemingly made to prove that shortly before the conflagration of the world, and the consummation of all things, a new revelation was to come to light, and a people arise, professing a purer faith, upon whom would be conferred the power of healing the sick, speaking in unknown tongues, and performing various other miracles.

This sermon was delivered with all that earnest fervor which usually characterizes the words and actions of him who is thoroughly convinced of the truth of what he utters, and deeply feels its importance. All seemed to listen with serious attention. The levity exhibited so unequivocally in the early part of the evening had all disappeared, and those who came for the purpose of making sport, and turning all the services into ridicule, returned home at the close of the sermon, silent and thoughtful. Some of the most respectable of the citizens came forward, and invited the preacher to visit that place again.

Upon the mind of no one, perhaps, was there made so profound an impression, as upon that of James Maverick. He knew the preacher, and he knew, also, the sacrifices, more cruel than martyrdom itself, which the preacher had made for that which he deemed the true faith. Though Maverick was far from being a Mormon, he could not avoid feeling a sincere respect for a man who had given such proofs of deep sincerity and regard for truth.

On their way home the subject of the sermon was discussed, and after their arrival, till a late hour of the night.

The next evening, Maverick attended the preaching. Night after night, for nearly two weeks, the Mormon held forth at the school-house of that settlement, to large and still increasing audiences. People came there from a great distance around, to hear the preaching. Much ex- {54} citement began to prevail. Five men, with their wives, all of whom were members of orthodox churches, came forward, and publicly confessed themselves converts to Mormonism. These were baptized by Mr. Wilmer, for the Mormons acknowledged not the validity of the rite performed by any sect or denomination. After this they were received into the church of the Latter-Day Saints. Other candidates were expected soon to follow. The opposition to Mormonism now broke forth with redoubled violence.

Good men looked on with fear and trembling, for no one knew where this delusion would end. None of the opposers of that sect were more implacable and unrelenting in their hostility to Mormonism, in all its various phases, than was Judge Maverick. He was a man of a sound head, and of sincere piety, but without a particle of charity for Joe Smith, or any intelligent man who preached his doctrines. He blamed his son James, severely blamed him, for harboring Wilmer, or listening to his preaching. Not even the hospitality shown to him by that man could justify him for inviting him to his house. The mother of young Maverick wept over him, and with anguish of heart implored him to avoid the Mormons, for it would "kill her and his wife both," she said, if he should be deluded by their sophistry, and join the odious sect. James was already aware of the feelings of Mary upon that subject, for, though she had forborne from speaking of the Mormons for a long time past, yet the increasing paleness of her countenance, and her dejected appearance, betrayed the deep anguish with which she beheld his frequent associations with the Latter-Day Saints. He was greatly affected at the sight of his mother's tears, for he had never before seen her weep as she did *now*, and solemnly promised her that he would go no more to their meetings, and hold no more intercourse with any of the sect.

The joy of his mother at this promise of her son was great. She went directly to his house, and communicated the intelligence to Mary, who was nearly overcome with this unexpected happiness. She embraced her mother-in-law, and wept tears of joy and hope upon her bosom.

Young Maverick faithfully kept his pledge, much to the grief and sore disappointment of Wilmer and the rest of the Mormons residing in that settlement, who had counted largely upon the weight and influence which *his* joining them would give to Mormonism in that region. He not only fulfilled his promise, but fulfilled it to the very letter and spirit in which he gave it, and refused even to listen to one of their ar- {55} guments. The only means they could employ to express to him their reproaches, was the silent look of sorrow and regret they cast upon him, whenever, by chance, he met any of their number.

He kept this engagement far more easily than he would have done, but for the circumstance that just at this important period Wilmer found it necessary to quit the settlement, and occupy a distant field, to which he was called by the imperative voice of the Prophet himself.

CHAPTER III.

"O! the happy days are fled;
    They never will return;
And the tears, to-day by Memory shed,
    Fall only on their *urn*."—*Moore*[1]

Several months have gone by since the departure of Wilmer
from the settlement of Sixteen Mile Prairie, in which period the
ever-varying features of Mormonism have assumed still another
hue. *"The Gift of Tongues,"* as it was styled, no longer confined
to one or two of their most popular preachers, had even become general. The most illiterate of their members, men and
women who were unable to read a single word of their own
native English, and even children, could prophesy fluently, it
was said, in Hebrew, Greek, Chaldee, Syriac, and numerous
other languages. This was now attempted at all their meetings.
Sometimes, the individual who uttered the strain of unintelligible sounds professed to give the meaning himself, in English;
but more commonly, the *"interpretation,"* as it was called, was
given by some one else. The excitement of the public mind was
manifested by scenes of violence which no native American
can remember without shame and mortification, for mobs and
lynch law became the order of the day. But these violent and
illegal measures had the effect which all attempts to change the
religious opinions of men by physical force ever have had. In
frequent instances, the meetings of the Mormons for public
worship, though held in their own houses, were broken up; and
fortunate indeed were the inmates if they escaped any worse outrage. In vain did the victims appeal for protection to the laws of
their country. Our institutions, which guarantee the freedom of
religious opinion to the Jew, the Mahometan, the Pagan, and

---

1. This is the opening verse of a poem titled "Confessions of an Old
Bachelor," which appears in the July, 1836, issue of *American Monthly*
magazine, 44–46.

even to the *Atheist*, afforded no protection to the Mormon. Their own dwellings might be invaded, their wives and daughters insulted and abused, their windows broken {56} in, and in more than one instance, their houses burnt down over their heads, with perfect impunity. Few magistrates will risk the certain loss of votes at the next election, merely to protect the rights of men without influence, against the injustice of the *multitude*, whether these hapless victims of mob law are Mormons or not.

The Latter-Day Saints increased but the more rapidly for these persecutions, and the consequence of it was, that proselytes were added to their church in nearly every place that their preachers visited. Some few of the Mormons, even at this early period, had lost their lives, and most of them held life and property only at the will of an American mob.

Under the direction of Joe Smith, the Latter-Day Saints had settled, in great numbers, in one of the counties of Missouri, high up the river of the same name. Here it was the intention of the Prophet to found a Mormon colony, which should become the permanent *"Head Quarters"* of the Order for all time to come. Many hundred families had arrived there from the various States of the Union, purchased a piece of land, and with great industry applied themselves to its cultivation. At the period of which we are now speaking, the people of that part of Missouri had, not long before, assembled *en masse*, driven these Mormons from their homes, and compelled them to leave that region. They gave them permission, however, to settle in a *new* and *uninhabited* county of the State, on the extreme frontier, adjoining the territory of various savage tribes, pledging their *honor* to the Mormons, that in that distant retreat they should never be molested.

Conducted by the Prophet, who marched at their head, always ready to share with his followers whatever toils and dangers awaited them, these Mormon Pilgrims, with their wives and children, and the scanty remains of earthly goods still left them, took up the long and melancholy line of their march to the Indian frontier. Here they applied themselves with the persevering industry that has ever formed a distinguishing trait in the character of the sect, and before many moons had waxed and wanted, every thing in that wild region had assumed a new and pleasing appearance. Each family had its own allotment of ground, upon which there soon arose a neat dwelling, and various other improvements.

But the Mormons scattered over the United States, most of them the newly made converts of preachers sent into the field, felt the hand of persecution, and in many places their lives were in great jeopardy.

To shield his people thus scattered abroad, was anxiously desired by {57} the Prophet. To effect that purpose, he resolved to call them all, with as little delay as possible, to that place, which he had established as the *"Zion"* of the sect. Smith had a new revelation from heaven, informing him that the time was now near at hand when the Destroying Angel would pass over the earth, when the wicked should be cut off in their sins, and the saints above possess the earth. Messengers were sent in every direction, where Mormon converts were found, to proclaim to them, in the words of the Prophet, "come out from among the wicked, my people, for why will ye perish with them—come up to the Zion which the Lord thy God has established for his saints." The unbelieving world, too, must be warned for the last time: *"get ye up, flee to the mountains, lest ye be consumed; for the great and terrible day of God's wrath is coming quickly, when the unbelieving world shall be utterly cut off."* Such were the messages to "saint and sinner," proclaimed abroad by the preachers sent out by Smith. Nor was the mission fruitless in converts. Instead of urging the people, as formerly, to embrace their doctrines, they now assumed a different tone, warning them *not* to join the ranks of the Latter-Day Saints, unless they were ready to lay down their lives, like the martyrs of old and seal the bonds of faith with their own blood. Other sects, said they, could repose on "flowery beds of ease," but the Latter-Day Saints have nothing to expect form the world but persecution and death. And this language was not without effect; for such is human nature, that persecution and bloodshed have always increased the persecuted sect. Employ force and violence to put down the wildest delusion that fanaticism ever invented, and you inevitably insure its success. The history of the world attests that truth. It is strikingly verified in the case of the Mormons. Hundreds who ridiculed the absurdities of that creed when its followers were unmolested, fell directly into the snare of Mormonism when their sympathies were awakened by seeing them calmly enduring persecution and death for the cause.

In all human probability, had the followers of Joe Smith been left to pursue the dictates of their own consciences, unmolested and undisturbed, as so many other religionists equally absurd have done, and yet do—in all probability, had not the Mormons been assailed with persecution, the plunder of their property by American lynch law, and made to suffer death—in all probability, the figment of the Golden Plates would long since have been forgotten, and the very name of Joe Smith perished from the memory of man. The wildest and most absurd {58} doctrines become *respectable*, when those who profess them seal their sincerity with their own blood.

Joe Smith, by standing firm and undismayed amidst the storm of persecution that beat upon his defenseless head, threatening death to himself, and utter extinction to Mormonism, called forth respect from even the most enlightened classes of society. One of the most talented of all our American poets said, in his thrilling *"Lines to Joe Smith,"* whose firmness in the fearful hour of peril had excited the admiration of the bard:

> "Not fallen!—no! as well the tall
> And pillared *Alleghany* fall;
> As well the *Mississippi's* tide
>   Roll backward on its mighty track,
> AS HE, THE CHOSEN's hope and pride,
>   The slandered and the sorely tried,
> In his triumphant course *turn back*."[2]

2. The poem that Russell cites here was written in 1832 by John Greenleaf Whittier. Its original subject was not Joseph Smith, but

The preacher sent at this time by the Prophet to the settlement in which Maverick resided, was a very aged man. His preaching could hardly fail of being eloquent, for the venerable form of the old preacher, and his locks, white as the driven snow, gave double force to the fervent appeals he addressed to his audience. New converts were made, and these, with the Mormons who had previously united with the Order, had decided, without hesitation, to obey the commands of the Prophet, and set out for Zion within a few months.

Maverick, true to his promise, attended none of their meetings, and held no intercourse with [t]he Mormons, but it was not possible for him to remain ignorant of their proceedings, for that subject was the theme of every tongue.

The effect which these affairs had on his mind was probably greater than it would have been, had he actually attended their meetings. He felt himself restrained from going among them by the promise he had given to his mother, and, in spite of all his efforts to prevent it, his thoughts would continually dwell upon that theme.

The old preacher often heard his brethren speak of the sore disappointment they had received in the desertion of Maverick. All had calculated upon his uniting with them, and his influence, they felt sure, would have led great numbers into the true fold. His loss was regarded as a serious calamity, and his defection was a source of deep regret to all.

The old Mormon, frequently hearing them lament his desertion, secretly determined that he would make a power effort to win him back to the church of the Latter-Day Saints. {59}

With that design, he visited young Maverick one afternoon, when he was at work alone in his field. He talked to him earnestly, but most affectionately. He told him of the revelation of

---

Henry Clay, who lost the 1832 presidential campaign to the incumbent President, Andrew Jackson. Russell changes Whittier's line "Ohio's giant tide" to "Mississippi's tide," and he changes "Columbia's hope and pride" to "THE CHOSEN's hope and pride." Otherwise Russell reproduces the first stanza of the poem verbatim.

the Prophet, that the destruction of the unbelieving world drew near. Warning him solemnly of his approaching doom, and expressing deep regret that the young man had not chosen his lot with the persecuted children of God, the Latter-Day Saints, the aged Mormon fervently and affectionately pressed the hand of Maverick for a moment, in silence and in tears; then solemnly bidding him an eternal farewell, left him.

The solemn air and manner of the venerable priest, no less than his warning and denunciation, went to the heart of Maverick like an ice-bolt. A cold, shuddering sensation seized him, and he felt like a felon suddenly and unexpectedly sentenced to death, from which there is no hope of reprieve. Twice or three times he was on the point of calling the preacher back, but in despair desisted. His mind was too ill at ease for him to think of resuming his labors, and he sat down listlessly, upon the plow which he had left there on the day previous. What would all his labors profit *him* or *his*? Of what use to him would be his fields—all his possessions—when he and they were so soon to be destroyed? He looked around upon his well cultivated farm with a sensation of inexpressible loathing. Had he not, for these, and for other earthly treasures, refused to unite himself with the people of God? What a price, what a fearful price had he paid, to console his mother, and still dearer relations! This passage of Scripture flashed like a scathing thunderbolt upon his tortured mind: *"He that will not forsake father and mother, wife and children, for my name's sake, is unworthy of the kingdom of Heaven."* Groaning aloud in his agony, he covered up his face, with the feeling that one so lost ought not to look upward. But, was it now forever too late for him to retract his rash and fatal promise? He knew not. Yet, even were it *not* too late, could he dash to the earth, at one blow, all the earthly hopes and happiness of his wife and parents, and unite with a sect which they detested, plunging them into sorrow for the remnant of their days? Would not his wife and child, like those of Wilmer, desert him? If they *did*, what a bitter cup would be pressed to his lips! Better die at once, than endure the long agony of an eternal separation from his wife and child. His mind was a chaos of harrowing thoughts. There he sat, unconscious of the progress of time, unconscious of everything but wretchedness, while the sun declined low in the west, and at last went down. The shades of twilight spread their dim curtain over him, and the chill dews of night had descended, when {60} he was aroused from his reverie by the voice of his wife, calling him by name. Alarmed at his long absence, she had sought him at the house of their nearest neighbor, and there learned that near sun-set he had been seen sitting down in his field, and thither she hastened, in the utmost alarm. The cold dews on his thin dress had chilled him, and when aroused by the voice of his wife, he shivered like one under the influence of the ague. To her anxious inquiries, he merely replied that he was unwell; begged her to feel no disquietude on his account, and accompanied her to the house. Mrs. Maverick knew nothing of his interview with the old preacher in the field, and had not the slightest suspicion that the subject of Mormonism occupied his thoughts. For several months he had attended none of their meetings, and avoided having any intercourse with the members, and most devoutly did she thank God that he had escaped their snares. She did not even dream that the fearful warnings of the old preacher, and his denunciations of impending destruction, at that very moment agitated her husband's mind, nearly driving him to frenzy and despair. She attributed his long stay in the field to sudden illness, and would have employed a neighbor to go for the physician, but this he peremptorily forbid, assuring her that he would be entirely well again after a night's rest. At supper, to quiet the fears of his wife, he attempted to eat, but the effort was beyond his power to accomplish. Food was loathesome to his sight. He drank part of a cup of tea, and retired to bed. Mary would have prepared for him some of the prescriptions which she had so often found efficacious, but he declined taking them. To avoid further importunities of his anxious wife, he closed his eyes and feigned sleep.

It was a long and dreary night to James Maverick. Every moment when awake, the warning voice of the aged Mormon was sounding its fearful knell in his ears, telling him of his doom. Every look, every gesture of the old preacher was still present to his view. The moment he fell into a slumber, the woes denounced upon him by the white-haired priest were all living realities, and their fulfillment was already begun. He saw the separation made between the *"sheep* and the *goats"*—the wicked cutoff—and none now remaining on the face of the purified earth but the Latter-Day Saints, who were the sole tenants of a sinless world, prepared for their residence alone.

In the morning, Maverick rose at dawn, and mechanically performed the usual jobs about the house. At breakfast he ate little, and his wife saw with alarm his haggard appearance. Shortly afterward, complaining of head-ache, he laid himself upon the bed. In an hour more, a {61} burning fever was raging in his veins. A messenger was sent to his parents, who immediately dispatched Frank for Dr. Horton, and set out instantly for the house of their son. When they arrived, James gazed long and earnestly upon his father and mother, but there was no intelligence in the glazed eye he cast upon his parents. He did not know them.

The doctor, on examining the symptoms of his patient, pronounced his disorder a *brain fever*, and immediately went to work, with vigor and skill, to combat the disease. He saved the patient's head, applied blisters, and employed other means of a depletory character. But vain hopes of his recovery were entertained by Dr. Horton.

For days the attendance of the physician was unremitting, except for an hour or two daily, when he returned home for a few minutes, and made a brief visit to a patient near by, who was convalescent, and out of all danger.

Little Eddy, at the commencement of his father's illness, was sent to the care of his aunt, that the undivided attention of his mother might be bestowed upon her sick husband. Judge Maverick passed the nights at the house of his son, and on his return home in the morning, Frank was sent there to assist his mother and Mary during the day, and that he might be present, should any unexpected emergency arise to demand his aid. These two women, the wife and the mother, were constantly at the bed-side of the sick man, except when exhausted nature required repose, when in turn they snatched a few hours of rest.

*   *   *   *   *   *   *

During the early part of his illness, Maverick neither spoke nor uttered a single word, or an exclamation of pain. He lay silent and still, his glaring eyes fixed, with frightful intensity, upon vacancy. His lips moved, at times, as if he were talking to the invisible being upon which he gazed, but no sound was heard.

At length, a change came over the suffering patient. He began to move restlessly in his bed, and at times muttered wildly and incoherently.

One night, during this period in his disorder, about an hour after midnight, Mary and Judge Maverick were keeping watch, alone, in the sick room. The mother, worn out with fatigue and anxiety, had retired to rest in an adjoining room. A neighboring woman, who had come there to watch for the night, finding it impossible to keep awake, had lain down upon the bed in which slept the elder Mrs. Maverick, and {62} was instantly fast asleep. All was still throughout the house, and not a sound was heard but the heavy breathing of the sick man. Suddenly he started—raised himself up in the bed, threw his naked arms wildly around, and cried out, in the most appalling tones ever uttered by mortal voice, *"The judgment! the judgment has come! Hark! its peal is sounding!"* At that very instant, a thunder storm that had long been rolling up unperceived by them, suddenly burst forth in a blinding flash, followed by a peal of thunder that seemed to shake the solid globe down to its very core. Mary heard something fall heavily behind her. Judge Maverick had fainted. But she had no time to attend to *him*, for her husband, in his insane ravings, was attempting to rise from his bed, and rush out into the storm that was now raging with violence. She dared not call aloud for aid, lest her cry should render the frenzy of her delirious husband uncontrollable. Seizing a pitcher of water that stood near her, on the table, she dashed its contents into the face of Judge Maverick, and instantly resumed her place at the bed-side of the maniac.

The Judge quickly revived, and sat up. Happily, the thunder clap awoke mother, who hastily put on her clothes and repaired to the sick room.

All the remaining part of that long, long night, the patient raved in delirium. It was now, for the first time, that his wife and parents became aware of the visit of the Mormon preacher to young Maverick, in the field. His ravings disclosed to them the startling fact, that the awful denunciations and warnings of the aged priest had unsettled his reason, and were still preying upon his life. In his delirium, the sick man repeated all that the Mormon had uttered, and often called aloud to the old man, imploring him, in the most moving terms, to have mercy upon him, and spare him from the doom he had pronounced.

In the course of the night, his ravings suddenly changed. He now imagined that father and mother, wife and child, had all resolved to leave him if he united with the Mormons, and he implored his wife, by the memory of their early love—by all his undying affection for her, and for their only child, not to cast him off. His supplications to Mary were heartrending, and almost beyond her powers of endurance, though she was fully aware that his entreaties to her were only the ravings of a disordered intellect. She threw her arms around his neck, and weeping upon his bosom, exclaimed, *"Oh no! no!* my poor, afflicted husband! I will *never* leave you, *never* cast you off, *never* desert you. In sorrow and affliction, in woe and misery, I will ever be yours. Father and {63} mother may spurn you, the whole world may scoff at you, my poor husband, but Mary will be your comforter. Even the wild delusions of Mormonism, that have so cruelly destroyed your reason, and made shipwreck of our happiness, shall not separate us. Like Ruth of old, "whither thou goest, I will go, and your God shall be my God." Should reason never again return to you, and I fear it never will, your head shall still be pillowed upon the bosom of your own true Mary, even *more* fondly than in the days of our early love."

While Mary was uttering these words, and for some minutes after, the maniac gazed so intently upon the face of his wife, that her heart thrilled with the hope that he at length knew her and comprehended what she had uttered. But her hopes were deceived. No lucid interval had yet dawned upon that disordered mind. On the contrary, his frenzy soon became still more wild and terrific. In the new mood of his delirium, he imagined that he stood, with the assembled universe, before the Judge of quick and dead, to hear his final doom. He had bartered the salvation of his soul, merely to please his wife and parents. The throng of glorified spirits who had triumphantly perished at the stake, or been torn in pieces by wild beasts, joyfully embracing martyrdom—all these, as they heard his story, turned upon him a look of withering scorn, and cried *"fool! fool!"* As the demons, at the command of his Judge, hurled him, shrieking, into the fathomless abyss, myriads of infernal shapes howled at him till every cavern of the gloomy vault echoed back the cry, *"fool! fool! fool!"*

He raved thus till near dawn, then gradually sunk into a calm and tranquil sleep that lasted many hours. Dr. Horton frequently went to his bed-side, during this interval, and anxiously examined the pulse of the patient, for this he believed to be the crisis of his disorder, from which he would rapidly recover, or immediately sink into the grave. There was another fear that haunted the mind of the doctor, which he dared not breath to others—the fear that his patient would become a confirmed maniac.

It was near the middle of the afternoon when the sick man awoke. None were in the room but the parents and wife of the patient, and Dr. Horton. He opened his eyes and gazed for a few moments upon the group at his bed-side, and inquired if he had been very sick. There was sanity of mind in that look, and every heart in the room beat with joy and thankfulness. Other questions from the sick man followed, all of which manifested a return of reason.

In a short time, at a sign given by Mary, all departed from the room, {64} and left her alone with her husband. She was anxious to remove from his mind, as quick as possible, the fear that she would abandon him, if he became a Mormon—a fear which she doubted not had caused much of the suffering and delirium he had endured. An hour passed by while she was alone with her husband. When she left the room her face was bathed in tears, and without looking at any one, she retired to her own apartment, bolted the door, as if to shut out her own thoughts, and throwing herself upon the bed, wept aloud. She had pledged herself to join the Mormons with her husband, go with him to the newly founded Zion of that sect, and, in weal or in woe, share the lot of her husband.

CHAPTER IV.

"And man, whose heaven-erected face
   The smiles of love adorn,
Man's inhumanity to man
   Makes countless thousands mourn."—*Burns.*[1]

Maverick now rapidly recovered. The old preacher had *triumphed.* The Mormons took no pains to conceal their exultation at having at length gained a proselyte who had so nearly escaped them, and one who would give so much weight and influence to the sect.

In about two weeks, James Maverick and his wife were baptized by the old Mormon priest, and formally received into the church of the Latter-Day Saints. On the pale face of Mary, as she stood by the side of her husband, on the bank of the stream in which they were immersed, resignation beamed, but not a single glow of that enthusiasm that shone in the features of her husband. Even the family of Judge Maverick believed that she had sacrificed her own happiness, to promote that of her husband.

*　　*　　*　　*　　*　　*　　*

It was now the middle of September, but the Prophet had given to the Mormonites of that *"stake,"* as it was termed, permission to remain till May, that they might dispose of their property. On the second day of that month, all the disciples of that region were commanded to set out for Zion.

The friends of James Maverick saw, with inexpressible grief, the ruin impending over his little family, and resolved to employ every {65} means in their power, during the few months preceding their intended departure, to convince him of his delusion.

Among the warmest friends of the Mavericks was a wealthy and highly accomplished English family, of the name of Stanley,

---

1. From the poem "Man Was Made to Mourn: A Dirge" by the Scottish poet Robert Burns (1759–1796). This is the first documented use of the now-famous phrase "man's inhumanity to man."

who resided about fifteen miles distant. Maverick and his wife had often visited them, and a warm friendship had sprung up between the two families. Great was the affliction of the Stanleys at the delusion of Maverick, and the self-sacrifice of Mary, for they knew the whole history of his conversion, and resolved to make an effort to save them from the ruin that awaited them.

An opportunity of putting that resolution into effect soon offered. Young Maverick visited them one day, with the ostensible purpose of returning a borrowed book, but with the real design of attempting the conversion of the family. The subject of Mormonism was soon introduced, and earnestly contested on both sides. At length, Maverick adduced the gift of unknown tongues as a proof of Mormonism, that was perfectly irresistible. He acknowledged that the gift had not been bestowed upon him, but Mr. French, a man with whom the Stanleys were well acquainted, often prayed in ten different languages, though ignorant of all but the English. *[*All that is said of French and Stanley occurred just as it is related.] The idea instantly occurred to Mr. Stanley to unmask this French, whom he knew to be an artful, but illiterate man, who loudly proclaimed his intention of going with his brethren to Zion, while at the same time he was buying up their farms at less than half their value, under a promise of paying the full worth as soon as he could dispose of them to advantage.

French had gained a fatal ascendancy over the unsuspecting mind of young Maverick, and Stanley believed that unmasking him would open the eyes of his friend. He told Maverick that French could easily palm off his gibberish upon the ignorant, but even French, with all his impudence, would not *dare* pretend, in *his* presence, to speak any language but English; and assured him if French would come there and utter a single sentence in any one of four languages that Stanley understood, he himself would turn Mormon.

This assurance of Stanley made a deep impression upon the mind of Maverick, whose confidence in the truth of his new creed was not a little shaken. He departed with a solemn promise to the Stanleys that he would abandon Mormonism, if French refused to come there and stand the test of praying in their presence in the "unknown tongues."

Maverick went directly to French, and told him all that had passed. {66} The wily fellow saw that he must play a bold game, or Maverick would escape from the Mormons. Numerous others would follow his example, and put an end to the speculation of buying their farms. Feigning the utmost willingness to stand the proposed test, he appointed an early day when he would go with him to the house of Stanley.

Great was the astonishment of that family, to see their young friend arrive in company with French. Mr. Stanley, unwilling to converse with the man upon any other subject, repeated to French the terms of his agreement with Maverick, and named again the languages in which he was to pray. French replied that it was impossible for him to say, in advance, what languages he might pray in, for he could only "speak as the spirit gave him utterance."

At his request, all present prostrated themselves upon their knees, and French commenced his prayer. After a few introductory petitions, he implored, with apparent fervor, the gift of *one* unknown tongue, to convince the unbelievers present. Continuing in that strain for a few minutes, he at length broke out into an unintelligible gibberish, the sounds of which were nearly all guttural. Then returning thanks for the gift of *one* unknown tongue, he implored the gift of another, and again uttered a string of unintelligible words, differing somewhat, in sound, from the former. For the fourth time he uttered what he termed an *unknown tongue*.

He had not spoken a word in either of the four languages named by Stanley, yet he evaded the force of this, by saying that he could speak only such tongues as the spirit dictated. Stanley stood aghast at the bold impudence of that impostor. It was in vain that he had attempted to undeceive Maverick. The readiness which French manifested to pray in the unknown tongues, in the presence of such a scholar as Stanley, removed from the mind of young Maverick the doubts which the arguments of his friend had excited, and served only to confirm him still more in that delusion.

The opposition to the Mormons, not only in that settlement, but all over the West, grew, day by day, more violent. Reports injurious to the sect, which had not the slightest foundation in truth, were everywhere circulated. Men who had hitherto been universally esteemed for their virtues, were accused, now that they had joined the Mormons, of every crime in the decalogue. Even Maverick was reported, at a distance, to be connected with a band of horse thieves, who united together, and protected each other from punishment by false swearing. Hardly a day passed in which he was not made the victim of some gross insult or abuse. {67}

These unmerited and cruel wrongs, inflicted upon that sect, and especially upon her own husband, made a deep impression upon the feelings of Mary. They enlisted her sympathies in the cause of the injured, and had a thousand fold greater effect than all the arguments of the Prophet himself could have had, to change her opinions. Insensibly to herself, the daily abuse unjustly heaped upon her husband wrought an entire change in her views of Mormonism, and she now joined heart and hand with that sect, and willingly united her destiny with theirs. Such is ever the effect of persecution, even of those most deeply in error.

The period of departure for Zion had arrived for the Latter-Day Saints of Sixteen Mile Prairie "*Stake*," and a very large company of them were to set out on the following morning. Maverick and his little family would pass the night at their nearest neighbor's. The articles most needed on the journey, and after their arrival, were already deposited in the wagon. Mary had carefully packed among these the few favorite play things of little Eddy, his magic lantern and his books. These were endeared to the heart of the youthful mother by many tender recollections, and she could not endure the idea of leaving them to other hands. Just on the eve of bidding a last farewell to the home she had so fondly loved, Mary resolved to visit it alone, when none could witness her tears.

The evening was mild, the heavens cloudless, and the air balmy with the odors of spring. The full moon had just risen, diffusing a mellow light over the landscape. Mrs. Maverick secretly left the house of their neighbor, to wander for the last time over her late peaceful home. She entered the deserted dwelling, and visited every room. She walked slowly among the shrubs and flowers that she had loved so well, every one of which had been planted and tended by her own hands. Many of them were now in full bloom, and almost seemed to look sadly upon her, whose care they had long received. These flowers and shrubs she would behold no more. She had now no home. Henceforth, she must be a pilgrim upon the face of the wide and unfriendly world. No hopes but such as spring from a faithful discharge of the stern duties of life were before her. Toil and suffering, and even martyrdom itself might be her lot. A few burning tears, which she could not repress, fell upon the flowers over which she bent. Quickly controlling these emotions, she knelt down among the shrubs and flowers, and implored strength from on high to discharge all the duties that might devolve upon her. She arose from her knees, calm and resigned, and {68} reached the house of their neighbor before her absence had been noticed.

*   *   *   *   *   *   *

We shall pass over the incidents of the journey to the Mormon Zion, and even omit the occurrences of the next two years after their arrival. Yet these two years were marked with signal events to the Mormons. Great numbers of the Latter-Day Saints had gathered there from the various States of the great American Republic, and some from nearly every Kingdom of Europe.

With the untiring industry which that sect has manifested at every place they have yet occupied, this wild frontier wilderness had been converted into fruitful fields. Smiling cottages had sprung upon every side, as if by magic. Each family had its own allotment of ground, and peace and plenty shed their hallowed influence around this community. The surplus products of their labor were exchanged with their merchants and mechanics for such articles as they needed, while their printing press gave them weekly intelligence of the far-off land which they had left, besides supplying them with books that taught them the laws and doctrines of their sect, with the revelations of their Prophet. Missionaries had been sent out, two and two, even into regions beyond the Atlantic, and hardly a place did they visit, which fai[l]ed of adding new converts to Mormonism.

But even here, where the Latter-Day Saints had come under a solemn pledge that they should not be molested—even here they found no abiding place. It was resolved to drive them from the region where their own labor had rendered valuable, or exterminate the whole sect. To justify this meditated outrage upon the rights of native born American citizens, the wildest tales were put in circulation against that people. They were described as thieves and assassins. Men of bad character, who had been expelled by the Mormons, gratified their revenge by publishing infamous reports. Strange as it may seem, one of the most effective means employed to inflame the public mind to the point of driving these people from the lands which they had honestly purchased, was the report that no Mormon could be punished for his crimes. It is quite probable that many, both in Missouri and Illinois, actually *believed* this charge; for we have yet, in these States as everywhere else, masses of dark, ignorant and uneducated minds, who are ready to credit any absurdity that can be invented. This same charge, that the Mormons could not be tried and punished, when guilty, availed to expel them from Illinois, but that charge is *false*. The man who asserts that criminals cannot be punished in our country utters a base {69} libel upon our republican government, and is unworthy of the name of an American citizen. To declare that under a republican government there is no power to punish robbery and murder—none to protect the innocent—is equivalent to saying that such a government as ours is *utterly worthless*. This is acknowledging the truth of the charges which the despots of Europe bring against our free institutions.

Nothing can be more false than the assertion, that the Mormons, of any other class of men, cannot be tried, and if guilty, punished. Every American, not profoundly ignorant, knows that when there is any fear that men suspected of crimes cannot receive justice in the county in which they reside, *the laws themselves* provide that these men shall be removed, for trial, to some county where *no such fear exists*. Will any base slanderer of our free institutions have the impudence to assert, that the people of Missouri and Illinois were so utterly corrupt and debased, that a single county could not be found in those two States, where the people were sufficiently honest to punish a Mormon, or any other criminal, if found guilty? The authors of these bloody outrages believed no such thing, for when Joe Smith, the Prophet and founder of that sect, voluntarily surrendered himself for trial in a county where *he* and the *Mormons* had not a single friend, did they try him? No! *He was basely, cowardly murdered in prison.*

It is often asked why it is that respectable citizens applaud these outrages, and other specimens of American Lynch Law, if these deeds of violence and blood are not *justifiable*. The answer is obvious. For the very same reason that respectable men in France applauded Robespierre and Marat, when in their hearts they loathed these monsters—*a want of moral courage*.

But we will return to the narrative of passing events, from which a desire to vindicate the republican institutions of our country from slander and abuse has drawn us.

Some dissensions had arisen among the Mormons themselves, and several families were on the point of abandoning the society, when intelligence came to Zion, that a large band of armed men was approaching that town, to exterminate them. In an instant every dissension was hushed, and those who, but a moment before, were at deadly feud with their brethren threw themselves upon their knees at the feet of those they had wronged, and with tears implored their forgiveness. There is nothing better calculated to unite people together, than the expectation of pouring out their blood as martyrs in the same cause.

The Mormon village was furiously assaulted on every side by an {70} overwhelming force. We are not writing the history of the Mormons, and shall give no details of that affair, except what belongs immediately to the Mavericks.

Mary, in the midst of the furious assault, continued to hide little Eddy behind the forge of a blacksmith shop that stood next door to their dwelling. Eddy, who had grown to be a boy of unusual intelligence and manliness of character for a child of his age, begged hard to be permitted to stand by the side of his mother, and share her fate, but this the anxious parents refused. Hardly had the boy been securely placed in that covert, when his father's dwelling was fiercely assailed, and Maverick, pierced with no less than four rifle balls, fell across his own door sill. Mary had just raised the head of the dying man in her lap, and heard his last sigh, when a cry of exultation rose from the adjoining blacksmith shop. Eddy had been discovered, and was dragged forth by a young man, whose real name we shall conceal under that of Vorne. Mary, with all the energy of her soul, implored them to spare her child, her only child, all that was now left to her widowed heart, pointing to her husband, who lay dead at her feet, in a pool of blood. But Eddy, even in this fearful hour, disdaining all supplications for his life, proudly drew up his form to its utmost height, and said, *"I am an American!"* Poor, mistaken, deluded child—he had read the history of his country, and vainly supposed that the very name of *"American"* would throw around his rights a shield of adamant. But the proud claim of the boy, and the wild pleadings of the young mother, were alike disregarded. Vorne replied, with a coarse, fiendish laugh, *"kill the young wolves, and there will be no old ones!"* Saying this, he coolly and deliberately brought his rifle within a foot of the child's head, and blew out his brains, sprinkling the clothes of the mother with the blood of her own child.

Let no one suppose, even for an instant, that the scene just described is a fiction. For the honor of manhood, we do most devoutly wish it were. But we assure the reader that every incident related, however, revolting, is strictly *true*. The slaughter of the father, the concealment and discovery of the boy, his proud claim, *"I am an American!"*—the reply of Vorne, and the blowing out of the child's brains before the eyes of the agonized mother, all occurred just as it is here related.[2] No human consideration would have tempted the writer to fabricate a fiction so revolting. But it is *truth*, and should be *told*.

With rapid strides we pass over the events that followed, for we could not dwell upon them without awakening painful emotions in the bosom {71} of the reader, and rousing against the perpetrators of these crimes the indignation of every true-hearted American, who prizes the free institutions of his native land.

We shall likewise pass over the tearless agony of Mary Maverick, who threw herself upon the dead bodies of her husband and child, and implored them in mercy to kill her also. Nor will we pause to describe her flight from her burning home, snatching only from thence a small bundle, containing a few articles rendered holy to her by the remembrance of little Eddy and her husband.

For an hour, the widowed, childless Mormoness fled into the wild forest, nearly bereft of reason. Overcome with fatigue, she sat down at the mouth of one of [t]he low, narrow caves so common in that upland region. Resting her weary limbs for a few moments, she tried to collect her thoughts, and inquire what were the claims of duty, even in that fearful emergency. Concealing her bundle as far as possible in that cave, with the intention of saving from the profane hands of strangers that which had been dear to her child, she departed, she knew not whither. Women and children equally forlorn were fleeing in every direction, with no aim but that of escaping, as fast as possible, from their assailants. Mary soon joined a band of these fugitives, and sought to forget her own sorrows in her efforts to console those

---

2. Though it is true that Charley Merrick, the model for Eddie Maverick, sustained a fatal injury at Haun's Mill on October 31, 1838, his death was not quite as dramatic as here described. He received three shots while trying to evade the mob and died about a month later while being cared for by his mother Philinda. Russell perhaps did not know the details, but it is more likely that he altered this scene for its dramatic effect.

whose afflictions were heavier than her own. Destitute of food and shelter, they dared not solicit either in the vicinity of their late residence, and these helpless outcasts endured untold sufferings. But, as they proceeded farther from the scene of their disasters, on their way to the Mississippi River, they found that compassion had not yet forsaken the humble heart. The sympathies of the better class of the people of Missouri were powerfully excited, and the doors of every respectable house on their route were thrown wide open to the sufferers. Their wants were supplied with a liberal hand, and no kind efforts spared to soothe their afflictions.

Though the public voice may sanction the outrages of *"Lynch Law,"* yet every really honest man execrates, in the secret recesses of his own heart, the lawless deeds that bring down reproach upon our free institutions, in foreign lands. Such was emphatically the case in the present instance, and sympathizing friends of the Mormons, as there would have done for any other sufferers, sprung up on every side. The most respectable people in Illinois took the lead in this manifestation of sympathy, and invited these homeless outcasts to settle in that State, on the bank of the Mississippi, not far from the town of Warsaw. This was the foundation of Nauvoo. {72}

Mrs. Maverick was everywhere received with the utmost kindness. She uttered no complaints, and never spoke either of her own wrongs and sufferings, or those of the Mormons, when she could well avoid it. She made no allusion, however distant, to her cruel bereavement of husband and child, but attempted to appear calm, and even cheerful, that she might hide from the world the sorrows which none could assuage. Yet a single glance at her pale, subdued countenance, told every observer that the iron had entered deep into her heart. There was a look of uncomplaining sorrow, mingled with the unfailing gentleness of her tones and manner, that touched the beholder. No one could see her, even in a crowd, without feeling a singular attraction toward the pale stranger. A young merchant of considerable wealth, and of high standing in community, at whose mother's house the young Mormoness found a shelter in the hour of her greatest need, felt that attraction irresistible. He offered to the homeless widow his hand and fortune, with the assurance that her religious opinions should ever be sacredly respected. This generous offer the Mormoness declined with profound humility, but decidedly, much as she esteemed him for his many virtues. All the promise that he could extort from her was, that she would accept from him any pecuniary aid that she might at any time find needful.

The Mormoness, feeling the impropriety of remaining any longer under the roof of her kind benefactress, after this declaration of her son, was compelled, once more, to go out into the world, and seek a new home. With the Latter-Day Saints she knew that she would receive a cordial welcome, but they had lost their all, and found it difficult to provide even for their own wants. She resolved, therefore, to return, as soon as possible, to the settlement of Sixteen Mile Prairie, and seek a home in the family of Judge Maverick, her father-in-law. Her thoughts had often turned toward them, and she knew full well that under their roof she would receive a heart-felt reception, as a daughter dear to their hearts. But she had long hesitated to return thither, fearing that the remembrance of other days, of her husband and child, would awaken, in that place, sorrows beyond even *her* power of endurance. But her heart had now been disciplined in the school of suffering and resignation, till at length she could look with calmness upon trials that would once have bowed her to the earth.

It was a lovely day in June, when she reached, on her solitary journey on foot, the borders of the settlement where she had formerly resided. A thin, fleecy cloud hung like a transparent veil over the sun, tempering his beams into the mildness of Spring. Numerous cattle {73} were scattered in groups over the vast prairie. Fields of wheat, fast ripening for the harvest, waved in the summer breeze, like the gentle undulations of a lake, whose bosom is faintly stirred by the evening air. Every object she beheld was interesting, from its association with other times. Even the buzzard, sailing high in air over the prairie, with no effort but now and then just dipping is broad wings, gave an air of quiet repose to the scene.

Many changes had taken place in the settlement, since the morning when, with her husband and child, she bade it a tearful adieu. New farms had been fenced in from the prairie, and happy children were playing around many a cottage that had risen up since her departure. Her heart throbbed painfully, in spite of all her efforts to restrain her feelings, as she approached the farm and dwelling that had once been *theirs*. It was a trial to which she had looked forward, and had endeavored to nerve her heart to meet it unmoved. But the effort was beyond her power. The dwelling in which she had once been so happy was now the residence of the wily French, whose influence over her husband's mind had been so injurious. There was the house, but all around it, how changed. The shrubbery which she had planted and loved to tend, had disappeared. All was destroyed, except the few broken remains of her former nurslings, that still survived the general wreck. At the door stood a boy of the size of Eddy, when he last roved, a happy child, among the flowers. But it was not *her* child. The sight was more than even *her* subdued heart could long endure. Turning her head aside, she walked on with a quickened step, breathing a prayer that God would forgive these murmurings of her bruised heart, and enable her to forgive all her enemies for the deep wrongs they had done her.

The reception which the wanderer received from the family of her father-in-law was deeply affecting. Judge Maverick, long accustomed, as he had been, to control his emotions in the presence of others, threw his arms around his afflicted daughter's neck, and wept aloud. Never before had even his wife seen him thus moved. The fountain of his sympathy was stirred to its lowest depth, and giving loose to his emotions, he sobbed like a child. He pressed the afflicted one long to his bosom, and, in a voice broken with mingled sobs, welcomed her to his home and to his heart, assuring her that so long as he had a roof to shelter her head, or a single crust to offer, she should be the dearest, most cherished object of his affection.

From the rest of the family Mary received a welcome equally kind and cordial, though less affecting. {74}

It was soon tacitly understood by all the household, that no allusion, however distant, should be made, in the presence of Mary, to the subject of her bereavement; and the neighbors who flocked in to welcome back the returned mourner were privately cautioned to make no inquiries about the death of her husband and child.

The family would have preferred that Mary should enjoy an entire exemption from all the labors of the household, and devote herself exclusively to reading and other literary pursuits; but to this she would not consent. She resolved to live usefully to others. Her afflictions had not, in her opinion, absolved her from the performance of a single duty she had ever owed to her fellow-beings. Only by aiding those who needed her assistance, by soothing the sorrows of the afflicted, and by enduring all the trials of life with holy resignation, did she hope to win the approbation of Him who had afflicted her for wise purposes.

Almost from the day of her arrival at the house of Judge Maverick, the Mormoness took upon herself no small share of the labors of the household. She rose at dawn, and was actively employed all day long. Her mother-in-law was an excellent house-keeper, but the industry and taste of Mary soon wrought a sensible change in the establishment. It was the earnest endeavor of the widow, not only to render herself *useful*, but to promote the happiness of the family, by appearing cheerful, and she anxiously avoided bringing up the remembrance of her sorrows to the minds of others.

For three months she remained here, performing most of the labors of the house. But though her step was light, and her voice cheerful, yet her pale, melancholy brow, and mournful eye, sunk deep into the hearts of the whole family. In vain did the kind, affectionate mother-in-law strive to banish from her mind all thought of the sorrows of the afflicted Mary. That mournful face, with its sweet, melancholy smile, was ever before her, and at length haunted her very dreams. The health of the mother-in-law began to decline, under this continual excitement of her sympathy. Mary was not slow in discovering the cause of the drooping spirits of her mother, and resolved to seize the earliest opportunity that would afford a plausible excuse for her departure, without rendering it necessary to assign ethereal cause.

Such an opportunity was quickly presented.

There lived in the neighborhood a rich widow, a foreigner, whose only daughter was in the consumption. They were Roman Catholics, strongly attached to their own church. During the year they had resided in the settlement, to try the effects of the pure air of the prairies, they had {75} enjoyed no opportunities of attending confession, or any services of their own church. Mary often watched with the declining girl, who soon conceived the most tender affection. As the life of this interesting girl waned toward its close, her thoughts turned more earnestly toward the world beyond the grave. During the long restless hours of night, she often conversed with Mary upon that theme.

The prayers and other services of the Catholic Church, were frequently read to her by the Mormoness, who felt no desire to interfere with the religious faith of any one, and least of all of the dying girl, who found in that her only consolation. As the last days of the invalid drew near, she became anxious that her mother should take her back to St. Louis, where she could receive the sacraments of her church, and her remains be laid in consecrated earth. The wishes of her daughter were sacred in the eye of Mrs. O'Dwyre, her mother, and Mary was earnestly entreated by the daughter to attend her. This request was granted. The departure of the young Mormoness from the house of Judge Maverick, was affectionate and tearful.

CHAPTER V.

"Truth, crushed to earth, *will* rise again;
    The eternal years of God are hers:
    But error, wounded, writhes in pain,
    And *dies* amid her worshippers."—*Bryant.*[1]

On their arrival at St. Louis, by slow stages, Mrs. O'Dwyre, to avoid the noise and tumult of a crowded street, rented a house on the borders of the town. For two weeks her daughter's health slowly declined, till her spirit took it flight. In her last moments the dying girl expressed her warm thanks to Mary, for all that she had done. Mrs. O'Dwyre continued to reside at the same place, and at her solicitation, the Mormoness consented to remain with her for a season.

In the vicinity of the house now occupied by Mrs. O'Dwyre, was a grove, in which there chanced to be encamped a small band of Indians, who had come from beyond the borders of Missouri, to transact some business with the commissioner of Indian Affairs, at St. Louis. Hearing that one of these Indian women was sick, Mrs. Maverick lost no time in paying her a visit. She found the poor creature not only dangerously ill, but suffering still more for the want of suitable attendance. She lay upon the ground, with nothing to protect her from the damp {76} earth, but a blanket. Two little girls, half-naked, cowered around the fevered couch of the mother. The squaws of the neighboring tents were not without compassion, but could render little assistance. Such scenes were once frequent. Formerly large bodies of Indians, nearly every year, encamped in the vicinity of St. Louis, to draw their annuities, or dispose of their furs.

Mary lost no time in procuring medical advice for the poor woman, and providing everything needful, and spent much of her time in attending upon her. The two little daughters were

---

1. From the 1838 poem "The Battle-Field" by the American poet William Cullen Bryant (1794–1878).

not forgotten. She furnished each with a new dress. These children were never before the owners of such beautiful garments,
and even Mary herself was amused at the looks of wonder and
admir[a]tion which they cast upon their simple, but neat calico
gowns. The dark face of the sick mother beamed with pride of
her children, and gratitude to Mary, as she turned her eyes from
one to the other.

The sick Indian woman, with the skillful attendance of the
Mormoness recovered. She owed her life to the kindness of her
white friend. Nothing could exceed the gratitude of the poor
squaw to her benefactress, and the thankfulness of her warm,
untutored heart was manifested with all the fervor of nature.
This band belonged to the half-civilized tribe of Shawnees, and
resided in the Indian Territory, beyond the borders of Missouri.
These Indians earnestly entreated Mary, whose history, by some
means, they had partly learned, to accompany them home, and
live with them. She could do so much good to them, they said,
and besides, could teach their daughters. They would build her
a house, even better than that of the missionary, and provide
for her support. The Indian whose wife Mary had tended was
an untutored savage, and said, "saved squaw's life—Indian no
forget—help make house for white squaw—hunt deer for her,
and anybody hurt white squaw, maybe he die quick."

The Mormoness, deeply impressed with the idea that her
labors would be useful to these Indians, and not unwilling to
withdraw from the society of the more civilized, accepted their
invitation. When Mrs. O'Dwyre discovered that it was vain to
try to persuade her from accompanying the Shawnees, she procured from a friend of hers a recommendation of Mrs. Maverick
to the kindness of the mission family. But, unknown to either
of them, a young merchant wrote privately to the agent of that
tribe, to supply Mrs. Mary Maverick with everything that might
add to her happiness, and draw upon him for the amount, be it
what it might. {77}

On their arrival at the Shawnee village, Mary took up her
residence for a time, in the mission family. The Indians, true

to their promise, set themselves earnestly at work to build her a house, and she was not a little surprised to find that it bid fair to be far the best in the village. The agent procured such materials and workmen as the Indians could not well provide. The house was large, for it was designed by Mary for a school, as well as for her private residence.

In a short time the Indians became warmly attached to Mrs. Maverick, who was constantly among them, wherever an opportunity of doing good presented. A few weeks of earnest application had enabled her to speak their language fluently, on all ordinary subjects, and this added much to her influence. With the girls who attended her school, it was a work of love to learn. Their dark faces beamed with confidence and affection, whenever [t]hey were turned toward their teacher, and she was known in the village by the Indian name which they conferred upon her, and which was one of the most affectionate terms in the whole compass of the Shawnee language. Every wish of hers was obeyed by these girls, and, unconsciously to themselves, they imitated her in everything, even in her gestures, and the tone of her voice. She sought to inspire them with a love for the *true* and the *beautiful*, as one of the most effective means of improving their minds. She adorned the yard of the school house with the shrubs and flowers that grew wild in that region, and it was deemed a sufficient reward to the most diligent and meritorious scholar, to be permitted to assist her in these recreations. The improvement of these Indian girls soon became visible in the neatness and taste seen in their own homes.

But even there, where the Mormoness devoted herself to the single purpose of doing good to others, without selfish thought entering her heart, she was not doomed to escape envy and detraction. Some whites oppose every attempt to instruct the Indians, because they deem it injurious to their own traffic. Even the family of the kind-hearted, pious missionary remembered that she was a Mormoness, and not all her deeds of charity and love could induce them to look upon her with entire cordiality. Reports, false and groundless, began to be whispered among the

Indians, and a few withdrew their daughters from the school. All this she met in silence, for she neither sought nor expected happiness from any other source than the consciousness of having faithfully discharged her duty, and no power upon earth could divest her of that. She had seen her husband and child weltering in their own life-blood, and had lived. After that, how trifling to her seemed every other affliction. {78}

At this juncture, a new and awful calamity assailed the Indians. The Asiatic cholera broke out in one of the largest and most powerful of the distant tribes of the West, spreading the utmost alarm, and threatening its utter extinction. The warrior, who had been the victor in a hundred fights, quailed at this new and resistless enemy. Great numbers died in a few hours after the attack, and consternation was universal. All who were able fled from the unseen foe, to seek protection among any of the distant tribes that would receive them. Whole families perished in their flight, and the unburied remains of the victims of that terrible scourge lay scattered over the plains. A party of near fifty, including men, women and children, fled to the Shawnees, who compelled them to encamp at the distance of two miles from their village. It was in vain that these savages had fled from the pestilence. Fatigue and terror predisposed them to the cholera, which broke out among them on their arrival, with redoubled violence. None of the Shawnees would visit their encampment, and none of the afflicted tribe were permitted to approach the village. To all human appearance, the whole encampment was doomed. In this emergency, the young Mormoness resolved to fly to the assistance of these friendless savages. No persuasion could shake her resolution. Procuring from the agent the few medicines prescribed for the cholera, she took a large bundle containing such articles as she would most need, and commending herself to the protection of heaven, she carefully closed the doors and windows of her house, which she might never again enter, and then departed for the encampment of the savages. On her way, she met the wagon of the mission family, who were hastening to the white settlements of Missouri. They paused long enough to reproach the heroic woman with *"tempting Providence,"* by rashly exposing her own life in such an enterprise. Unmoved by this denunciation, steadfast in her purpose, she resolutely pursued her way. Death, in the frightful form of cholera, might await her, but, whether life or death was to be her lot, she felt that the path of duty was always the path of safety, and the only one.

Great was the astonishment of these savages, when they saw a female of beautiful form, apparently twenty-four or five years of age, in a snow white attire, suddenly appear among them, and, in the Shawnee tongue, inform them that she came to attend upon their sick. The smile with which she announced this unexpected message, gave to her pale countenance an expression such as they had never before seen; and this, with the fact that no one had seen her approach, inspired them with the belief that she was not a mortal. The Great Spirit, pitying his red children, {79} had sent down, to succor them in their distress, one of the "Daughters of the Sun." They would have thrown themselves at her feet, had she not, by a gesture of the hand, forbidden it. Joy and hope now took place of the dark and sullen despair into which they had been plunged. The Mormoness went instantly to work in aid of the sufferers. The Indians cheerfully obeyed her orders. She had the sick removed into a large tent, where she could have them all under her eye at once. Eagerly did they swallow the nauseating drugs that she administered, without a word of inquiry, and in full confidence of recovery, for they believed there was life in every medicine administered by her hand. Calmly, and with a light, quick step, the young Mormoness moved among the sick, giving medicine to one, wiping the cold, clammy dew from the forehead of another, and holding to the fevered lips of a third the cooling draught. To all she spoke words of hope and consolation, that cheered and comforted their desponding hearts.

In a few days, the sick were all convalescent. None had died since her arrival, except those whom she had found in the last stages of that fearful disorder. They now began to be in want of the necessaries of life, and the Shawnees still prohibiting all communication with the village, Mary dispatched a trusty messenger to her house in the night, to bring from thence her whole supply of provisions, which, happily for them, was not a small one.

Ingratitude is not among the vices of savage life. It is only in the society of the *civilized and refined*, that man repays the kindness of a friend and benefactor with hatred. These Indians made no loud and boisterous professions of thankfulness to the Mormoness, but gratitude, deep and heartfelt, beamed in every look they gave her. One of her patients was a savage of powerful frame, regarded among them as the bravest warrior of the tribe. None who recovered was so violently attacked with the cholera as he. For some time he lay motionless, and apparently insensible, but, though unable to move, or articulate a word, he observed every movement of his kind nurse, and saw the untiring efforts she made in his behalf.

In the very first day that he was able to leave the tent of the sick, and return to his own, after a short absence he came back and stood directly before the Mormoness. He held in his hand a large bundle carefully enveloped in a neatly tanned fawn's skin, and said, in his broken English, *"Pale-faced squaw saved Wahhe-yah's life—give her Great Medicine—great much."* Slowly unfolding the package, which Mary doubted not was some trifling object which the Indians are ac- {80} customed to adopt as their *"Medicine,"* or *Manito*, what was her astonishment, when the last envelope was removed, to discover the very bundle of little Eddy's play-things, which she had hidden in the cave when fleeing from her burning home. *"Wah-he-yah saw pale-face squaw at cave."* Saying this, the savage drew close to Mary, and in a low tone he uttered, between his teeth, a name that made the Mormoness start, and a livid paleness overspread her countenance. It was the name of Vorne, the murderer of her child—not the name *we* have given him, but his *real* name. With a look of revenge and hate glaring in his burning eyes, which seemed like those of the incarnate demon of vengeance, the warrior added, *"Wah-he-ya know him—pale squaw much cry—maybe! ha! ha! ha!—maybe—ha! ha!"* and with these unintelligible exclamations, he left the tent.

Mary wept long over her recovered treasures, now the dearest object she had in existence, for they once belonged to her child. They were [t]he very play-things which she had so often seen him play with, when he was a careless, happy child, and she a happy wife and mother. They were all that was now left her of those happy days, and where is the bereaved mother who will not enter into her feelings, as she gazed upon these newly re-covered relics? Yes! her husband and child had gone to a bloody grave, without the form of a trial, and that, too, in a Republic that guarantees to every individual unlimited freedom of con-science, and a fair trial by jury—a Republic upon whose flag is emblazoned the Roman Eagle. Wherever the banner of Rome played in the breeze, *there* the meanest citizen found protection. Paul, the Apostle to the Gentiles, the preacher of a sect abhorred and accursed by the multitude, found instant protection under the wings of that eagle. When he calmly, but proudly folded his arms upon his breast, and said, *"I am a Roman citizen,"* the haughty Satrap trembled on his throe, for well did he know, that if he dared violate the rights of the meanest, most criminal of her citizens, Rome, in the language of one of her sons, *"would hurl at his devoted head a thunderbolt."* But does the American eagle thus protect the rights of the free-born citizens of our Republic? A voice from many a Mormon grave, from the blaze of unnumbered dwellings, and from the victims of Lynch Law in numerous other forms, answers this question. It tells, trumpet-tongued, the protection which our institutions afford to the un-popular citizen, who most needs protection.

Mary remained with these savages till the last patient had recovered, and the band was preparing for their departure, when she re- {81} turned once more to her own house, with the inten-tion of again opening her school. She was received with every demonstration of joy. Her brief absence had taught them more fully her worth, and even the parents who had withdrawn their daughters confessed their errors, and sought to repair the wrongs they had done her. In a few days, her cottage was again liberally supplied with every needed provision.

The sorrowful Mormoness, who thought no earthly happiness could ever reach her, was destined to receive an unexpected joy, most welcome, and most dear to her heart. A brother whom she had not seen since she beheld him on his departure from her father's roof, a mere lad, had now grown almost to manhood, and sought out his afflicted sister, whom from his infancy he had fondly loved. It was his intention to try to persuade her to return with him to the home of their childhood. We will draw a veil over the meeting of this brother and sister, after so long a separation.

On the second day after his arrival, Mary and her brother visited a sick family, who resided a short distance out of the village. The day was beautiful, and instead of returning immediately home, they continued their walk along what was termed the "Shawnee trail," till the last habitation was left far behind them, for Mary wished to show to her brother some of the wild scenery in that region. They were conversing earnestly together upon the subject of her returning home with her brother, when a cry of mortal agony, that paralyzed all their faculties, rang through the still air. Again and again, for the third time, that cry burst forth in tones that froze the blood in their veins, and then all was still. In the next moment, a horse with saddle and bridle, but no rider, rushed wildly by. Hastening in the direction from which the animal came, they discovered, at no great distance a man lying upon the ground, in a pool of blood. As Mary drew near enough to distinguish his features, she started back aghast, horror-struck. Every lineament of that upturned face was engraved upon her heart, in lines that time could not obliterate. She had seen it often in her dreams. The wounded man was *Vorne*, the murderer of her child.

With a powerful effort, she controlled the emotions which a sight so revolting to her, inspired, and stooping down, stanched the blood that flowed from three deep, and apparently, mortal wounds.

While she bent over the wounded man, she heard a voice from the adjoining thicket, which she recognized, in an instant, as that of the savage warrior. *"Ah ha, maybe!"* was uttered, and then followed the Indian war-whoop, the yell of victory. He had paid what in his savage {82} code he regarded as a debt due to his benefactress. He had laid her deadly foe prostrate in death, and, with the feeling that he had done a good and noble deed, he departed to join his band, already on their march, and at no great distance from that spot.

The wounded man, though insensible, was not quite dead. He had evidently been shot from his horse with an arrow, and received several stabs with a knife after his fall, any one of which seemed mortal.

Giving her brother no intimation that she knew the name of the wounded man, or had ever seen him before, the Mormoness had no difficulty in procuring his aid and that of others, to remove him to her house. Besides the deep wounds which the apparently dying man had received, the loss of blood was so great that the least unfavorable turn in his case would inevitably be fatal. Such was his weakness, that he fainted several times on his way to her house, and nothing but the most vigilant care on her part enabled him to survive the agitation of his removal. The exhaustion which he endured was so great, that for hours after his arrival he lay upon the bed insensible. Two long weeks of intense suffering to the wounded man, and of constant watching, day and night, alternately by Mary and her brother, passed by before the vigorous constitution of Vorne triumphed, and a decidedly favorable change took place. All the thoughts and emotions of the wounded man were now no longer concentrated upon his own sufferings, and he began to feel an interest in other topics. At first, every inquiry was answered by forbidding him, in his weak condition, to converse. As he grew stronger, this prohibition was unavailing, and Mary found it necessary to acquaint him with the condition in which he was discovered, his removal to her house, and, in short, answer all the numerous inquiries that he made upon various other topics. Vorne was deeply sensible of the disinterested goodness of his benefactress, and gradually drew from her all of her past history that she chose to relate, which, indeed, was little more than the fact that she was a Mormoness and a widow, with no pecuniary resources, but depended upon the avails of her own labor for support. But she carefully concealed from him that she had once resided at the Mormon Zion, in Missouri, and everything relating to the death of her husband and child.

Out of all danger, his wounds healing daily, he had full leisure to turn all his attention to what was passing around him. Confined to the narrow limits of a sick room, the most trifling events become interesting to an invalid. Vorne observed every movement of the young widow, and saw with what anxious and unwearied attention she watched over {83} him. He thought of all she had done for him, and was conscious that to her disinterested kindness and energy he owed his life. If she had not watched over him for many days and nights with a devoted attention which few sisters would bestow upon a brother, he would now be sleeping in his grave. Her pale face soon became the engrossing subject of his thoughts, as it had long been the most pleasing object that ever met his view. To him there was something peculiarly attractive in her manners, and the sound of her light foot-step, hardly audible to any one else, made his heart beat with a quicker pulsation. These emotions every day grew more and more intense, till his whole being—every passion of his soul—was concentrated, with fearful strength, upon her alone.

He had hitherto regarded the marriage institution with the scorn and contempt which men of base lives and corrupt principles always conceive for that relation, but now—he resolved to marry the widow. She was a Mormoness, but when once his wife, he could easily compel her to abandon her religion. He had accumulated a small fortune by his dishonest trade with the Indians of various tribes, and he would enjoy it in one of the old States, far from the reach of the avenging arrows of those whom he had defrauded. He determined, however, not to disclose his feelings to the young widow till he had entirely recovered. But the burning passion that was now consuming him he had no longer the power to control, and all his previous resolutions yielded to the anxiety to learn his fate at once.

One day, when Mary's brother had started to go on an errand for his sister, about two miles distant, and would not return for some hours, Vorne seized the opportunity of declaring to her his passion, and asking her hand in marriage.

It was some time before the Mormoness fully understood his meaning, so foreign from all her thoughts and expectations was the bare idea of such a declaration. When she fully comprehended the meaning of his words, no language can describe the loathing and horror which filled her whole soul. The man who had mocked at her wild, agonizing, heartrending plea for the life of her child—the man who blew out that child's brains before her face, had asked her hand in marriage! The very thought of it made her recoil with horror. Never before had she felt for Vorne the unutterable loathing which she now endured. No, not even when the cold-blooded remorseless ruffian stood in triumph over the bloody corpses of her husband and child, did she feel for him such unutterable horror and detestation as she did now. Her {84} whole frame quivered with the intensity of her emotions, her bloodless lips moved, but no sound escaped, and her hand was involuntarily thrown out, like one in the nightmare, who seeks to ward off some terrific monster. Vorne gazed upon her in mute surprise, yet, so far from suspecting the nature of her emotions, he ascribed the wildness of her appearance to the unexpectedness of the proposal, which his overweening vanity told him could not but be highly gratifying to a widow as poor as she was, and a Mormoness besides.

The door opened, and Mary's brother, who had met the man he was going to see, entered. The spell in which all her faculties seemed bound was instantly dissolved, and drawing a deep sigh, like one just awakened from a hideous dream, she rushed from the room.

The command, *"Love your enemies, do good to them that persecute you,"* were no unmeaning words in the creed of Mary Maverick, and she earnestly endeavored to fulfill the precept, and feel for her remorseless persecutors the spirit of Him whose dying prayer for his murderers was, *"Father, forgive them."*

The trial of attending upon Vorne, which before, Mary, at times, found hardly endurable, was rendered doubly irksome by this declaration. But still, it was her duty to *forgive*, and render good for all the deadly wrong he had done her.

She now carefully avoided being in the presence of Vorne when her brother was absent, and thus afforded him no opportunity of renewing his revolting proposals. But she could not always have the protecting presence of her brother, and about a week after the scene just related had transpired, he found her alone, and again made the offer of marriage. She was now prepared for the [e]vent, and preserved a command over her feelings. Without giving him any intimation of her acquaintance with any portion of his previous history, she mildly declined his proposal, alledging no other reason than her determination, her unalterable determination, never again, under any possible circumstances, to marry.

Greatly was he disappointed, for he had entertained not a doubt of her willingness to exchange poverty for comparative affluence. He combated her resolution with every argument that he thought might have an influence upon her mind. Remembering that she was a Mormoness, the idea struck him that her objections arose from that source, and he professed great esteem for that sect, and promised that he would himself join them. To gain her hand, he hesitated not to promise to unite with a sect which he had persecuted to blood. {85}

When he found that even *this* did not shake her determination, he broke out into a storm of passion, in which deadly threats were mingled with professions of love, almost to frenzy. Refusing to accept her refusal as decisive, he told her that he would give her a week for reflection upon the subject, at the close of which he should expect her *final answer*. To this she agreed, and would have again assured him that neither time nor any circumstance could change her mind, but this he prevented her from uttering.

On the return of her brother to the house, Mary took him alone, and, having first obtained from him a solemn promise that he would not attempt to avenge her wrongs, she informed him that Vorne was the murderer of her child, and acquainted him with his proposal of marriage.

We will not describe the emotions of the brother. It was enough that he had sworn not to avenge his sister, and the murderer should be left for punishment to the tribunal of Heaven.

The wounds of Vorne were rapidly healing, and in a week more, if no unfavorable symptoms should arise, he would be able to remove from there with perfect safety.

It was settled between the brother and sister that their patient should depart on the day appointed by himself for his final answer.

The week whose hours were so anxiously numbered by all the inmates of that dwelling slowly rolled by. The morning of the day arrived on which Vorne expected a final answer. From some cause or other, he had become doubly confident that after a week more or meditation upon the ills of poverty and dependence, her answer would accord with his own wishes.

Hardly had breakfast been dispatched on the morning of that eventful day, when a summons came for Mary to attend the bed-side of a dying woman. It was near sun-set when she returned. Supper passed by without any allusion to the subject. With trembling anxiety, the Mormoness saw the shades of night descend, and the dreaded crisis draw near. Her heart beat violently as she lighted the lamp and placed it upon her rustic stand, which she drew to the middle of the room. Having done this, she retired for a few moments to her own apartment, to collect her thoughts, and implore the protection of the Most High.

On her return, her brother, who had been present all the morning, arose, and, in compliance with the previous arrangement which he had secretly made with his sister, left her alone with Vorne. His departure {86} from the house afforded the latter an opportunity most ardently desired, of conversing with the widow alone.

After a pause of a few minutes, during which the Mormoness could almost hear the beating of her own heart, Vorne introduced the subject ever present to his thoughts. He told his love, and told it in burning words. That he felt for the widow all the deep and absorbing emotions of which his wild, impassioned nature was capable of feeling, was no fiction. Her gentleness of soul, so unlike his own, her soft, pensive, melancholy air, and her unceasing kindness to him during the long days and nights when his life hung by a thread, had awakened in his turbulent, impassioned bosom an affection for the Mormoness, which he felt would be the ruling passion of his soul to the last hour of his existence.

To this ardent profession, the Mormoness calmly, but firmly gave a repulse. Not even yet believing her decision unalterable, he spoke of her unprotected condition after her brother should depart, and of the wealth he had acquired by trade. As he proceeded, his voice rose with the increasing excitement of his mind. He at length adverted to her connection with the Mormons, and his generosity in proposing to unite himself with one who belonged to a denomination so unpopular, so abhorred by the public. He would take her to a far distant State, where her former connection with them would be forever unknown.

In the excitement of his feelings, he had unwittingly confessed his deadly hatred to a sect which he had proposed to join, and, unknown to himself, touched a cord that vibrated to the profoundest depths of her heart, and brought before her mind's eye, in all the vivid hues of truth, the fatal scene when her agonizing prayer for the life of her child was received with a fiendish scoff.

Even *then*, anxious to spare the murderer pain, she told him again that her resolution was unalterable, and begged him to depart in peace. Not satisfied with this, he still sought to shake her resolution. It was not till then that the Mormoness, finding other means of no avail, told him that there was an obstacle to her union with him—a barrier between them, wide and impassable as the gulf of fire that separated the rich man in the Gospel from the bosom of Abraham—and again most earnestly implored and entreated him to depart in peace, without making any further solicitations or inquiries.

A storm of passion arose in the bosom of Vorne, and broke forth wildly and fearfully as the hurricane of the tropics; and he *demanded*, in the most violent manner, to know what that obstacle was. Know it {87} he would, and trample it down, even at the risk of his life. The Mormoness, alarmed at his violence, arose from the table, with the intention of leaving the room. Vorne instantly sprang forward to detain her by force, and, in his attempt to seize her arm, overset the lamp and extinguished the light. In an instant, a sight met the view of Vorne which riveted him to the spot, as if he were transformed into a marble statue, and his eye-balls glared with intense horror. On the opposite wall of the room, directly before him, he saw the Zion of the Mormons. It was noon-day. An armed mob, most of whom he instantly knew by name, rushed along the principal street. Across the door-sill of a cottage lay a man, weltering in blood. The scene changed. A youth, hardly twenty-one years of age, in whom Vorne recognized himself, was dragging a lad of noble bearing before the door where lay the dying man, the child's father. A lovely female who stood by the side of the bloody corpse, appeared to plead in agony for the life of the child. He now knew her face in an instant. It was the woman who had watched over him with more than a sister's care—the woman to whom he owed his life. He saw the young man spurn the imploring agony of that mother, and deliberately blow out the brains of her child. Every scene was so true and life-like, it seemed to Vorne a living reality.

All was now explained. Everything was now clear to him as noon-day. It was *her* child that he had murdered, without imagining that killing a Mormon would ever rise up against him. He it was who had wantonly bereft that woman of her last hold upon life. And knowing this, and bea[r]ing the wound every moment in her bosom, she had devoted days and nights to his recovery. All this pas[sed] through his mind with the swiftness of a flash of lightning, and writhing with anguish of soul which few beings on earth are capable of feeling, he exclaimed, *"O, I am accursed of God and man—my punishment is greater than I can bear!"*

The brother of the Mormoness came into the room with a light, and led his almost inanimate sister to her own apartment, and instantly returned. Stepping to the outer door, he called into the house of an Indian, who stood without, holding Vorne's horse, which was equipped for a journey. Then addressing himself to the latter, he said, "Vorne, your horse is at the door—all your things are deposited in your saddle-bags—this man will conduct you to a house, which is not far distant—you can pass the night there, and in the morning pursue your journey—depart in p[ea]ce." Vorne listened to this speech like one but half awakened from sleep, and mechanically followed the Indian. Without the pow- {88} er of bidding adieu, or of uttering a single word, he left, forever, the house, where, for a long period, he had received every attention in the power of kindness to bestow. On the ensuing morning, at the earliest appearance of light, he arose from his sleepless couch, mounted his horse and before the sun had risen above the long line of forest which bounds the distant landscape on the east of Shawneetown, he had left that village miles behind him, on his way to the States.

The exciting events of the past night had not been unfelt by the Mormoness. The death of her husband and child, with the sorrows through which she had passed, were all presented before him, and she felt as if she had been wading through that troubled sea for the second time.—Her long confinement at the bedside of the wounded man had already impaired her health so seriously, that her constitution was unable to withstand the rude shock which the last night had given her.

The means by which her brother had thrown these vivid representations upon the wall, by the aid of the optical instrument so cherished by his sister, in memory of her child, needs no explanation. The views were painted by herself, long after the occurrence of the events they portrayed, and were true to the life. Every feature of those scenes was too deeply traced upon her heart ever to be obliterated.

In the morning a fever was preying upon the life-blood of the Mormoness. In a few days it left her, for the fuel that sustained its fires was consumed, and a languor, the unfailing harbinger of approaching dissolution, pressed with leaden weight upon her heart. She felt that her days were numbered, and the summons was one of joy to this daughter of affliction. Since that fearful day when all she held most dear was torn from her embrace, but one hope, one aim, one object of life reconciled her to existence. Henceforth she lived only that she might do good to others, confidently trusting that the afflictions through which she might be called to pass, like a fiery furnace, would purify her heart. To do good to her enemies, to return the anxious care of more than a sister to the man who had bereaved her of an only child, she hoped would be acceptable to Him who prayed for his executioners.—Daily did she feel the influence of sanctified afflictions descend upon her heart, gentle as the dews of Hermon, fortifying her in the discharge of all her duties, and preparing her for Heaven.

The last mournful scene, the welcome release to this woman of many sorrows, was near at hand. She prayed for all her friends and relations. For her mother, in the far-off home of her childhood, her own fond mother, upon whose bosom she had so often slept, for her she pray- {89} ed with an earnestness which touched every heart. She prayed fervently for the Mormons, and for their persecutors, and for all who had wronged them or her. And now she felt that she had done with the scenes of earth, and stood on the confines of the spirit land.

For many minutes she lay motionless, her eyes closed. The pulse at her wrist had ceased, and not the slightest breath stirred the light down of the feather held before her pale lips. All thought her spirit had departed. Suddenly she opened her eyes, and gazing upward, her arms extended as if to clasp some object dearest t her heart, she exclaimed, in tones of rapture, *"Husband! Eddy!* I come! Receive me again to your bosoms, my husband and child! I come! I come!" Uttering these words, the lone sufferer was at rest, and, we trust, received a crown of rejoicing from Him whose command is, *"Love your enemies!"*

Three weeks after his departure from the Shawnee village, Vorne was discovered in the vicinity of St. Louis, wandering about like one who is bewildered, or who has lost his way. A relative of his took charge of him and his effects. In a short time it was found necessary to chain him to prevent him from committing suicide, which he had twice attempted. For many days and nights he sat sullen, muttering wildly and incoherently to himself about the Mormoness, after which a change came over his disordered mind, and he raved and howled in the most fearful manner, and his friends were compelled to consign him to a mad-house. There he yet remains. The physicians who have attended upon him have not the slightest hopes of his recovery. Wild raving, hopeless remorse, like the vultures of Prometheus, are ever [g]nawing at his heart. The murder of the boy, and the agonized supplication of the mother, are ever present to his mind. Nor has even insanity torn from his mind a single act of kindness which the afflicted woman had bestowed upon him who had bereaved her. He remembers it all—his own crimes, and her heaven-born charity in returning good for evil—and he will remember it forever. When he has passed the confines that divide earth from the spirit land, the memory of his crimes will survive fresh and green forever.

John Russell, of Bluffdale, Illinois.
(By S.G. Russell.)

Among the many that the tide of emigration swept from Vermont to the "far west," was John Russell, of Bluffdale, Greene county, Illinois.

He was born at Cavendish, Windsor county, Vermont, on the thirty-first day of July, 1793. He was the son of John Russell and Lucretia Preston. His father was an old-fashioned Baptist preacher, severely Calvinistic in his belief and puritanic in practice. His mother, like Dorcas of old, was renowned for her piety and good works. He had one brother, older than himself, Bliss by name, and one younger, Elias, and three sisters, all of whom he survived, save one sister, Sally, who married David Perkins. Polly married Levi Jackman, Eunice married Dr. Joseph Gray. His parents were in very moderate circumstances, and could give their children no educational advantages, save what they could gather at the common schools during the winter months. John, however, had an inordinate thirst for knowledge, as most of his ancestors had been college graduates, teachers, preachers and writers; he determined to try for a better life than that of a small-fisted farmer, on the mountain slopes and huckleberry hills of old Vermont. So, contrary to parental advice, and almost contrary to parental command, he entered Middlebury College, March 25, 1814.

He had already commenced authorship, in order to acquire the needful funds for his collegiate education. His first literary venture was "The Authentic History of the Vermont State's Prison," a duodecimo volume of ninety pages; only one copy of which is known to be in existence, and that is in the archives of the Vermont State Historical Society. In the preface of his modest volume, he says: "It is not the unpardonable vanity of becoming an author but necessity, the mother of invention, that produces the present volume." The sale of the copyright of this book, materially aided him in his first year in college. Without any parental assistance, aided by only a few benevolent hands and by the feeble efforts of his pen, he encountered difficulties and obstacles, which very few would have had the persistence and hardihood to have resisted. This little book was published at Cavendish, Vermont, in 1812, by Preston Merrifield, with whom he had in earlier years, served an apprenticeship at the bookbinder's trade.

This book binding experience he very rarely referred to in after life, though he became a proficient in the business. Merrifield had a cow, and father said, "when the cow came up, they had mush and milk, and when the cow did not come up, they had mush." Yet his remembrance of Merrifield was always of the kindest.

The sale of his book, and the never failing recourse of indigent students – school teaching, carried him through the freshman and sophomore classes. Through the other two classes, he was assisted by William Slade, a young lawyer of Middlebury, and for whom father always cherished the most grateful feelings. Slade afterwards became the Governor of the state. Many years afterwards, while father was living in St. Louis county, Missouri, and in prosperous circumstances, he repaid Slade both interest and principal for all of his timely assistance.

During the interval between the junior and senior classes he taught school at Vergennes, Vt., where he not only became acquainted with my mother, but made a profession of religion and united with the Baptist church. He had hitherto been atheistic in his belief, led thereto by the rigid Calvinistic faith and stern puritanical practice of his father.

Upon his return to college he found himself the only Baptist student connected with the college.

He graduated in 1818. Soon after, he went to McIntosh county, Georgia, and commenced a school, but on account of his anti-slavery views he ended his school rather abruptly.

He had, during his teaching at Vergennes, Vt., become engaged to my mother, in fact, she was one of his scholars. On leaving Georgia he started after my grandfather and family, who were emigrating to the "far west," and overtook them at Whitewater, Harrison county, Indiana, where they had encamped for the winter, and here he was married to Laura Ann Spencer, on the 25th day of October, 1818, by one Mainwaring, who was a justice of the peace and a minister of the gospel. In the spring of 1819, he removed with his young wife to the Missouri Territory. Here, in St. Louis county, he became tutor to Augustus and Marcus Post, sons of Justus Post, then a prominent man in Missouri, for which service he received a salary of five hundred dollars per annum. Here he wrote his immortal "Venomous Worm," which, a few years after, John Pierpont, of Boston, Mass., introduced into his National Reader, as also did the McGuffies in their series of readers. After his tutorship had expired, which was about 1825, he taught school in the city of St. Louis, then only a small French town. In 1832 he taught a high school at Vandalia, Ill., then the capital of the State. Here he became intimately associated with James Hall, author of "Harp's Head" and many other literary works. Hall was then the editor of the Illinois Monthly Magazine, for which father contributed some of his best literary productions.

In 1833 and '34 he taught in the Alton Academy, which afterwards, by the endeavors of John Mason Peck, became Shurtleff College.

While living in "Bonhommie Bottom," Mo., he became intimately acquainted with John M. Peck, who was at that time at the head of the Baptist denomination in the west. The friendship was closely and warmly cherished during their whole lives.

In 1828 he removed from Missouri to a farm in Illinois (now occupied by the writer of this sketch), to which he gave the beautiful name of Bluffdale, and in the following year, Oct. 9, 1829, he was appointed postmaster by Postmaster General McLain, which office has continued on his farm ever since, de[s]cending from father to son (now 1900).

On the 9th day of February, 1833, father was licensed to preach. His license is signed by Elijah Dodson and Sears Crane, ministers, and David Woolley, clerk. His natural timidity and retiring disposition prevented him from ever being ordained; he had no confidence in himself – only in his pen.

In 1837, '38 and '39 he edited *The Backwoodsman*, at Grafton, Illinois, of which Paris Mason was the publisher and proprietor. For this paper he wrote "The Specter Hunter," "Cahokia," "Ellwood, the Outlaw," and "Sir William Dean; or, the Magic of Wealth."

In 1841 and '42 he was editor of *The Louisville Advertiser*; here he became intimately acquainted with Richard M. Johnson and George D. Prentice, the poet. At first he and Prentice were bitter political enemies. Prentice was editor of the *Louisville Courier*, which was intensely whig, while the *Advertiser* was democratic. Prentice threatened several times to challenge "Old Bluff," as he called father, but mutual friends interfered and he and Prentice became, as long as life, literary friends.

Father was principal of Spring Hill Academy, at Clinton, parish of East Feliciana, La., for about six years, also superintendent of public schools. For two years, (1849–50) he taught the High School in Carrollton, Ill., when he retired from public life to his farm, and devoted himself exclusively to writing for the press.

For the Baptist Publication Society of Philadelphia, he wrote, "Alice Wade," "Going to Mill," "Lame Isaac" and "Little Granite," for the copyright of which, he received quite a sum of money. All of these have been stereotyped and may be found in a catalogue of their publications. About this time he also wrote "Claudine Lavolle" and "The Mormoness," "The Drama of Human Life," "The Emegrant" [sic] and "The Lost Patent," besides filling the Baptist papers week after week and year after year, with articles on all subjects, for which he hardly received thanks.

From his early manhood he was a bitter opponent of African slavery and some of his vainest efforts were leveled at the "divine institution." His letters to "John Kelly, born in Massachusetts," attracted national attention. John Kelly was a "Missouri Border ruffian" in the Kansas troubles, and one of the most insanely devilish, of all of the cut-throats of that trying time; and publicly boasted that he was born in Massachusetts. Father more than "skinned him alive," along with others of his ilk. His articles were published in the *St. Louis Intelligencer*. Many attempts were made to discover the author, but in vain, the editor kept the secret well.

In 1843, he returned home from Louisville, Ky., and found that the "wolf of hell," in the form of one Chandler, a half Atheistic, half Universalist preacher, had broken into the little fold of the Baptist church, and badly scattered the flock. He began preaching to the remnant of the flock, and finally, preached a sermon against the Universalist Salvation, from the text "Thou Shalt Not Surely Die," so hot and caustic that it made him so many bitter enemies, of those whom he had been accustomed to call brother, that he gave up preaching and went back to Louisiana, and went once more to teaching. I.M. Peck was at our house soon after the sermon was delivered, and father showed him the manuscript; Peck put the MSS. in his pocket, and its subsequent publication, with Peck as editor, was the outcome. The little book is entitled "The Serpent Uncoiled." It went through three editions and was in its time popular. In Little Granite, he had Governor Bissell as his hero. Bissell and he had long been friends.

About 1831, he wrote for the Illinois Monthly Magazine an article entitled "Three Hundred Years Hence." It was in the form of a dream and set forth what this country would be, three hundred years hence. Among other predictions, he dreamed that the river at St. Louis was spanned by a bridge. He ends his dream by saying, that if any one did not like his dreaming, he gave them full right to do their own dreaming.

Thomas Lippencot, who wrote under the *nom de plume* of "Salem," as my father did under that of "Bluffdale," in a criticism says, that he thinks that Bluffdale rather overdone the thing even for a dream, in dreaming a bridge across the turbulent, boiling Mississippi at St. Louis!

After that the Eads bridge became a foregone conclusion, Judge N. Ranny wrote to me to enquire if a copy of that dream was yet in existence, and if so, requested a copy for publication.

I answered by sending him a copy. It was reprinted in the Missouri Republican and read at the dedication of the bridge.

When the Mormons were driven out of Missouri, in 1838, by mob violence, Sidney Rigdon, Parley Pratt and a number of fugitives stopped at our house for shelter and hospitality. Father heard from them the heartrending stories and barbarity of the cut-throat Missourians, hence came the story of "Mary Maverick, the Mormoness." In this book he has not overstated or exaggerated a single fact. The Rev. Mr. Merrick was a Baptist preacher and preached in Missouri and Illinois in early times, but was finally led astray, and went over to the Mormon faith (the wife of whom was the Mary Maverick of the story.) In their retreat from Missouri, he and others being closely pressed, took refuge in a blacksmith's shop, but they were betrayed, and captured, and shot down like dogs. His only son, a lad of eight years of age, had hidden under the bellows, but was dragged out by a ruffian; the boy bravely cried out, "I am an American citizen! I am an American citizen!!" but the Missouri barbarian put the muzzle of his gun to the brave boy's head and blew his brains out; the women they let go, and Mrs. Merrick came back to Illinois to her friends, and not to Nauvoo, for she was not herself a very bigoted Mormon.

Now to relieve the sadness of the story, I will relate an anecdote of this same Merrick. Like a great many at the present time, he was very boisterous in his declamation, making much more noise than was absolutely necessary. Mother said, that one time after father had heard him preach, that he got up in the night and wrote something on a slip of paper. It was this:

> Good Brother Merrick may screech and may holler,
> As if his lungs wasn't worth more'n six bits or a dollar;
> But of his throat and his lungs he'd best have a care,
> For his church is too stingy to buy a new pair!

In 1832 and '33 father was Sunday school agent, employed by some eastern society. He planted Sunday schools in almost all the counties in Southern Illinois.

My father was a small man, about 5 feet 6 inches in stature, with dark auburn hair, large, deep blue eyes, and of a very light complexion; he was of a cheerful, jovial disposition, very fond of a good joke well told; some of his best productions were of a humorous nature. Only a few of his most intimate friends knew the whole worth of his generous heart, his pure manhood, his patriotism, and more than loyal friendship. His intercourse with the world was marked by the most childlike gentleness. His simple reliance upon Providence, his unshaken faith in the power and efficacy of prayer, have marked with a ray of Divine light, his pathway down the rugged ways of life. His love for children was more than womanly in its tenderness; he never saw a child however humble and obscure, however unkempt or unwashed, but that he had a pat on the head for him, and a kind and cheerful word. He was the beloved playmate of all the ragged urchins in the neighborhood, and his kindness had left its mark upon their hearts; for many of them as they gathered around his coffin to take their last look upon a face that never met them without a smile – wept with a sorrow that would not be pacified.

Kind hearted as a woman, he would not have needlessly set his foot upon a worm. The poor and unfortunate, whatever might be their character, he never turned empty away from his door. He was generous to a fault, impoverishing himself that he might cast plenty into the lap of those he loved. Putting implicit confidence in the integrity of all mankind, he was over-reached in almost every pecuniary transaction, as careless of worldly wealth as he was grasping after the wealth of science.

Few have been more ardently devoted to the welfare of the whole world, more earnestly striving for the liberty and education of all that bear the image of God.

He died on the 21st day of January, 1863. He died of old age; his close application to books and book making had worn him out prematurely.

Though his illness was severe, yet his death was calm and serene, like flowers at set of sun. He died with all the confident hope of a true Christian; he was not afraid to trust that God whom he had loved and served for fifty years. His last spoken words were "confidence! confidence!!" After he could no longer speak, he wrote upon a slate, "see that Brother Bulkley's children have some apples." Justus Bulkley, D.D., preached the funeral sermon from Ecclesiastes chapter 2, first and second verses.

Bluffdale, Green county, Illinois, May, 1900.

P.S. – I should have said in this sketch that the old Chicago University conferred upon John Russell the degree of LL.D., with which he was in his old age much more gratified than he would have been in his younger days. Father told me that for a long time he had had the idea of the "Venomous Worm" in his head, but had not yet committed a line of it to writing. That he had agreed with the editor of the "Columbian" to write two or three articles for his paper, in payment of his subscription, and that the editor had called upon him for one of the promised articles, and that he sat down and in less than the quarter of an hour he committed "The Venomous Worm" to paper; that it was but once copied from the original draft, and that at that time he had no idea that he had written an article that would outlive all else that he had written or would write. Mr. Brown, editor of the Alton Courier, told me that he read "The Venomous Worm" when a school boy in the Highlands of Scotland. It has been rendered into poetry several times, and the authorship attributed to several different ones; and it has been published in all the temperance almanacs, and many temperance papers, both in England and America. John Knapp, editor of the Missouri Republican, was very anxious that I should say that it was first published in his paper, and offered me a life subscription if I would so assert. The Columbian was a small paper published at St. Charles, Missouri, in early days.

S.S.R.

John Russell to Thomas Gregg, July 7, 1841[1]

Bluffdale July 7th 1841

My Dear Friend,

Since I wrote I have received yours, and as I make it a point to answer all your letters—"here goes." Yes, the price of the mag. is too low. When the prosp.[ectus] for subscriptions is published, it will be two dollars. Mr. Peck entreats me to wait two weeks longer, before I issue the prospectus. He has a different plan in his head. If the mag. goes on, you, of course, must write, and not "free gratis for nothing". You shall receive, per page, the same that I make. A neat little effusion, such as no one knows better than you how to write, does a great deal for such a work. I could name some of your pieces that would do credit to any periodical in the English Language. You know the proverb, "what man has done man can do again."[2]

You speak in your last, also, of the Mormons. You would not give your opinions upon a subject on which you were not willing that I in turn should give mine. I shall, therefore, in the spirit of that friendship that has so long subsisted between us, give you my sentiments, frankly. If you believe that I would on no account give offense to you, let me say you will believe truly.

I do most sincerely regret the course you are pursuing towards the Mormons. I do not believe that it is your intention to excite a mob against these deluded fanatics. No, I do not. I know

---

1. John Russell and Family Papers, 1792–1927, box 1, folder 6. Abraham Lincoln Presidential Library and Museum, Springfield, Illinois.

2. Russell and John Mason Peck had recently written a prospectus for a historically themed periodical to be called the *Monthly Magazine of Early Western History*, to which he was inviting Gregg to contribute. However, for some of the reasons articulated in this letter, the proposed publication never materialized.

the kind heart that beats in your bosom too well to believe <u>any such thing</u>. But you could not pursue a more direct course to affect that object, if such <u>was</u> your design. Of this opinion every reader of the "Signal" will bear me out. It is no difficult task to kindle up the fires of persecution against that sect. The rabble in your county, as elsewhere, would gladly engage in the work were public opinion such as to screen them from punishment. You are fast bringing public opinion up to that point. I fear that even now, through the influence of the "<u>Signal.</u>"[3] Nauvoo has already been deluged in blood. If God has given me any talents as a writer, most fervently do I implore Him never to leave me to employ my pen to promote intolerance, or array the vilest of our race against any sect, however friendless and derided it may be.

Do you remember the indignations that rolled in flashes from your pen about the Alton mob? Why, and whence, the change that has come over you, on the subject of persecution? I never had a doubt but Beecher induced Lovejoy to pursue a course that Lovejoy's better judgment condemned,[4] but still you can not point to a line of mine in which I approved of the mob. I frequently impressed upon my readers that a mob never <u>was</u>, and never <u>could be</u>, justifiable.

Let me tell you an incident that will more fully explain my views. There is a family about two miles from this that are <u>deservedly</u> <u>unpopular</u>. Some months ago a party of men were resolved to lynch the man. Though that family have spared no efforts to injure <u>me</u> and <u>mine</u>—were the deadliest enemies we ever had, and I believe are our only ones, I volunteered to defend that

---

3. The *Warsaw Signal*, with which Gregg was affiliated, had taken a strong anti-Mormon position under the editorship of Thomas Sharp. When Gregg took over editorship of the *Signal* in 1842, he changed the name to the *Warsaw Messenger* and substantially moderated its attacks on the Mormons.

4. Elijah Lovejoy (1802–1837) was an abolitionist writer and printer who was killed by a pro-slavery mob in Alton, Illinois, in 1837. Henry Ward Beecher (1813–1887), a well-known writer and social activist, was present at the riot as Lovejoy's supporter.

cabin or die. By immediate and vigorous exertions I awakened such a spirit in this settlement that the mobocrats dared not make the attempt. I should act precisely on the same principle with the poor deluded Mormons. I think of Joe Smith just as you do, and I believe that a greater knave walks not the face of the earth, yet were I there I would defend his hearth-stone with my blood. Joe Smith is an American citizen, and shame on the people—all that can tamely stand by and see the sacred rights of any American cloven down.

My neighbor had deeply wronged me, but I could not see my own rights—yours—and those of every American trodden into the dust in his person.

Now what excuse can any one render for exciting the populace against the Mormons? Is it because their religious creed is erroneous? It would make even "the weeping Philosophers" burst into a loud laugh to be told that a mob has such a sacred regard for the religion of Christ that it prompts them to plunder and murder. True, the creed of the Mormons is erroneous and I, who am a Baptist, do most sincerely believe that there is error in the doctrine of the Presbyterians, Episcopalians, Methodists, etc. etc., nor dare I think that the Baptists themselves are exempt. I doubt not the pure eye of Jehovah sees error in every sect and in every individual of evert sect. God has compassion on us, and let us exercise compassion towards the errors of our fellow sinners.

"The Signal" assigns the reasons why you assail them, that they wish to monopolize all the offices in the county. Do they indeed!! Well, that is nearly as bad as we Whigs in Greene. Last summer we made every possible exertion that time, money, and talent could make, to monopolize every office in our own party. To be sure, our opponents called us every thing that was bad for so doing, and pursued the very same course with better success. In this they did just what is such an unpardonable sin in the Mormons. The Locos[5] believed that if we gained the victory we should destroy the liberty of the country, and we Whigs believed

5. The "Locos," or Locofocos, were a New York-based anti-Tammany Hall faction of the Democratic Party in the 1830s. During the 1840

(I did and yet do) that if Van Buren was elected our country was gone. If there is no other charge against the Mormons it is hardly worth while to bother them yet awhile.

I am sorry to say that the course pursued for months past by the N.Y. "Evangelist" and the Baptist "Pioneer" explains the whole business. How long is it since these two papers labored hard to get up a persecution against the Catholics—and to give currency to a book fit only to be read in a brothel, and which those editors knew to be false?[6] Each of these editors are as zealous to build up their own sect as Joe Smith can be to build up his. Human nature is the same everywhere, and in every age. The same spirit that hung the Quakers and imprisoned the Baptists in New England, and disenfranchised every man that did not belong to the Presbyterians or rather Congregational Church, is yet alive, and it is that spirit which induces the Evangelist and Pioneer to raise up a mob to destroy the Mormons. Let me tell you that I have not a doubt but that the Signal will destroy the settlement and town of the Mormons. I am fearful that on opening the next number I shall see that event announced in starring capitals. But the excitement will soon fade away and the deepest feelings of sympathy be awakened for that people. Their errors will all be forgotten in their sufferings.

Well I have written frankly, and I trust from good motives. I would not have touched the subject at all had I not felt it to be my duty. Had I not written to you, and the Mormons had

---

election, Whigs such as Russell used the term as a general name for Van Buren supporters and the Democratic Party.

6. The *New York Evangelist* was a prominent Presbyterian newspaper in New York City. *The Pioneer* was a Baptist newspaper in Illinois edited by Russell's friend John Mason Peck. Both papers were influential in publicizing the 1836 anti-Catholic book, *The Awful Disclosures of Maria Monk, or, The Hidden Secrets of a Nun's Life in a Convent Exposed.* This book presented itself as the memoirs of a Canadian nun who escaped to the United States after years of sexual abuse (luridly described) by priests in the convent. It was soon shown to be a hoax, but it remained popular for much of the nineteenth century.

been plundered and butchered, I should never have silenced the reproaches of my conscience. Whether I have any influence with you or not, I have discharged my duty. Come what may, I have done the little that lay in my power to do. I can do no more. I shall not again even allude to the Mormons. My letters hereafter will be upon more pleasing subjects.

Let me hear from you soon, so that I may know that you take no offense. No offense I assure you is intended.

Respectfully and affectionately,

J. Russell

From *The Serpent Uncoiled*[1]

{43}

CHAPTER III.
ABSURDITY OF UNIVERSALISM.

The Doctrine of Universal Salvation contrary to Reason and the Common Sense of Mankind.—Its Pleas examined—1. That God is Love; 2. That Conscience is a sufficient punishment. 3. Universalism contradicts the Voice of Conscience; 4. Human Tribunals and the Dealings of Almighty God.—Universalism not taught by Christ and his Apostles.

It is contrary to the plainest dictates of reason and common sense, to believe that a holy, sin-hating God regards sin and holiness alike; and all denominations, some of the Universalists included, agree that God abhors sin. Can the Holy One of Israel look with the same complacency upon the remorseless ruffian whose hands are often steeped in human blood, as he does upon the saint who walks humbly with God, and devotes his whole life to doing good? If there is in reality a difference between these

---

1. For the origins of *The Serpent Uncoiled* see Appendix A, page 75 : "In 1843, he returned home from Louisville, Ky., and found that the 'wolf of hell,' in the form of one Chandler, a half Atheistic, half Universalist preacher, had broken into the little fold of the Baptist church, and badly scattered the flock. He began preaching to the remnant of the flock, and finally, preached a sermon against the Universalist Salvation, from the text 'Thou Shalt Not Surely Die,' so hot and caustic that it made him so many bitter enemies, of those whom he had been accustomed to call brother, that he gave up preaching and went back to Louisiana, and went once more to teaching. I.M. Peck was at our house soon after the sermon was delivered, and father showed him the manuscript; Peck put the MSS. in his pocket, and its subsequent publication, with Peck as editor, was the outcome. The little book is entitled '*The Serpent Uncoiled*.'"

two characters, God sees and knows that there is a difference, and his conduct must conform and correspond with that fact. To deny this, is to deny that He is a God of truth. When a {44} thing is true, God never acts as if it were not true, as man too often does, for all His acts are truth and holiness. Either there is no difference in the sight of God between sin and holiness, or else God in his dealings with man makes the same difference between them as actually exists.

SECTION I.

The plea that "God is Love, and therefore will not afflict or punish the wicked," examined.

This argument, if it may be called an argument, is one that no Universalist preacher fails to advance on almost every occasion in which he attempts to prove his doctrine, and to many it has proved convincing. We will therefore examine it. They contend that as God is our Father, and that He is love, he could not endure to inflict even so great a degree of suffering upon his creatures as earthly parents could upon their children, because His love is infinitely greater. We readily grant that the love of God for man is indeed infinite, or he never would have sent His Son to die for our redemption. Yet this by no means proves that he will {45} not punish those who reject his offers of pardon, and despise his grace. A king might justly be said to love his rebel subjects who were justly condemned to die if he offered them all a free pardon, nor would it prove that he did not love them if he punished those who chose to be punished rather than accept of pardon, notwithstanding his earnest entreaties.

God is love, but he is also just. The Bible gives us no reason to believe that he is so weakly compassionate as to be unjust. It is for the highest good of the universe that intelligent creatures should be governed by a being who is just in all his ways. He cannot love the universe supremely unless he is strictly just in all his dealings. It is a contradiction in terms to say, that he loves man so well that he cannot do justice. Had not a way been opened so that he could have received and accepted those that believe in Christ and yet be perfectly just, not a soul would ever have been saved.

So far from being so compassionate that he cannot inflict suffering, the Bible tells us of numerous instances in which even in this life he inflicted upon the wicked the most awful punishment. In the days of Noah, with the exception of eight persons, he destroyed the {46} whole human family from off the face of the earth. Upon Sodom and Gomorrah he rained fire and brimstone.

We ourselves see that even those who have not been guilty of any uncommon crimes are often called to endure the bitterest afflictions. How many are born blind, or deaf, or dumb, or deformed, or idiots? Great numbers are afflicted all their lives long, with incurable diseases, racked night and day with pain. How large a portion of the human race were swept off some years ago by the Asiatic Cholera? Great numbers are annually struck dead by lightning, perish by shipwreck, or the explosion of steamboats. How many are destroyed by earthquakes. In a single town in the West Indies, the town of Point Petre, several thousands lost their lives not long since by that awful visitation of God.[2] Not a few, including men, women and children, were partly engulfed in the earth, or buried under the ruins of fallen buildings, and lingered days and nights in untold agony before death came to their relief.

How many have perished by famine; and not a small proportion of the whole human race, even in the present age of the wo[r]ld, endure all {47} the ills of extreme poverty, from the hour of their birth to that of their death.

The sinner who builds his hopes of escaping future punishment upon the belief that God is so compassionate that he cannot endure to see men suffer, builds his hopes upon sand. If we daily see that he inflicts even upon the righteous the keenest sufferings that man can endure in this life, what reason have we to conclude that He cannot inflict sufferings still keener and

---

2. The Guadeloupian city of Point Petre was completely destroyed by fire in 1770 and by earthquake in 1843. It is the latter event that Russell has in mind in this 1846 publication.

more enduring in the life to come, upon the wicked who reject his offers of pardon and scoff at all his mercies?

We know that God does all things well, though we may not understand all his motives. We know, however, that He afflicts the righteous for their own good. Afflictions wean their hearts from earth and draw them near to God. The Psalmist says, "before I was afflicted I went astray." "Every son whom he loveth He chasteneth,"[3] are the words of inspiration. {48}

SECTION II.

The plea that Conscience inflicts in this life all the punishment that sinners deserve, examined.

This is a favorite dogma of the Universalists, and one upon which they place great dependence. They discourse eloquently about the awful punishment which conscience inflicts, and contend that it is always in proportion to the sinner's demerits, all that he ought and all that he will endure.

To refute this plea, the aid of Scripture is not needed, for it will be fully refuted if held up to the light of reason and common sense.

So far from punishing the wicked according to their deserts, conscience, by repeated acts of wickedness, becomes seared as with a hot iron, and in a great measure ceases to perform its office. Many a man who has wronged his neighbor to the value of a dollar, feels more remorse of conscience than does the hardened pirate in making a whole ship's crew "walk the plank" into the ocean. How often it hap- {49} pens that men who have grown rich by fraud and oppression, live and die without feeling enough of the sting of conscience to induce them to restore a farthing of their ill-gotten gains. If the doctrine that conscience inflicts in this life all the punishment that crime merits is true, then must it also be true that the more crimes a man commits the less does he deserve punishment; for it is evident that the pious, godly man, who mourns over his shortcomings, feels far more of the

---

3. Psalms 119:67 and Hebrews 12:6.

upbraidings of conscience than does many a remorseless ruffian whose hands are steeped in blood.

But, stop a moment. Supposing that all mankind really believed that every one goes straight to heaven the moment the breath is out of his body, would conscience be very troublesome to them, think ye? Would it whisper to them fearful things about the worm that never dies? Would it alarm them by telling them of the judgment day, and of the awful sentence, "depart ye cursed, into everlasting fire, prepared for the devil and his angels?" NOT AT ALL. Nothing of the kind would conscience whisper to those who really believed the doctrine of universal salvation, and all ought to believe it if true. On the contrary, {50} it would tell them that they are safe from all punishment hereafter, and will go right to heaven when they die, though they have robbed the widow and the orphan of their last crust, and steeped their hands to the elbows in innocent blood. Would such whisperings of conscience as *that* be very difficult to bear? Would they be so agonizing, think ye, as to be a sufficient punishment for the most atrocious crimes? Would it be intolerably agonizing for a villain to believe that after he has revelled all his life long upon gains procured by blood and crime that he will go immediately to heaven when he dies, there to enjoy endless happiness, and that not a question will be asked him about his sins? I ask, candidly, if he believes this, whether conscience would be apt to trouble him very much?

Who does not see that if the doctrine of universal salvation was believed by all mankind, conscience would be divested of all its power to inflict punishment; and yet, strange inconsistency, the believers in that doctrine contend that conscience inflicts in this life all the punishment that sinners merit. {51}

SECTION III.

The doctrine that all mankind go to heaven is contradicted by the voice of Conscience in every human bosom, with the exception of the very few who believe that doctrine.

There is not a nation or tribe of men, however wild or savage, of which we have any account, and who have any notion of a future state, that do not believe in the endless punishment of the wicked and the endless happiness of the good. They differ as widely as possible as to what will constitute the happiness of the one or the misery of the other; yet all agree that it will be endless, and infinitely greater in degree than anything that can be experienced in this life.

Among the thousands of heathen tribes in Asia, Africa, America and the unnumbered islands of the Pacific, the objects of worship are greatly diversified. Some worship an alligator, some a bird, some an ox, some an ape, and some a log of wood. Hardly an object, animate or inanimate, can be named that has {52} not been worshipped by some heathen tribe or other. Now, how does it happen that amid all this endless variety, in which hardly any two nations worship the same object or practise the same rites—how does it happen that all these different tribes agree in believing in the endless happiness of the good and the endless misery of the wicked, when they agree in little else? How shall we account for this striking fact, except by believing that God has impressed this important truth upon their consciences, or revealed it to them in some way?

It is true that in this Christian land there are many who profess to disbelieve the doctrine of future punishment; but conscience could never have taught them this, for it requires a long effort before any one can divest himself of the belief of future punishment, and it is doubtful whether any ever believed the doctrine so thoroughly, that doubts of its truth did not frequently arise in their minds. {53}

SECTION IV.

If the doctrine of Universal Salvation is true, then not only all human tribunals, but the dealings of Almighty God, would seem to be contrary to the plainest dictates of reason and justice.

The criminal code of every nation on earth recognizes the principle that the punishment of death is the greatest that man can inflict, and the greatest that man, in this life, can endure. Many accounts are given in scripture, in which Almighty God, for crimes of a very deep dye, punished the offender with death. Now, if all go immediately to heaven when they die, then were these criminals *rewarded*, not punished.

Let us see how the dealings of Almighty God correspond with the doctrine of universal salvation.

The old world was steeped in iniquity, till their wickedness called for the sorest punishment. But eight righteous persons were found. So God took these wretches immediately into the joys of heaven, because of their extreme wickedness—took them to heaven as a punish- {54} ment for their enormities; but pious Noah, on account of his piety, was doomed to remain on earth. Korah, Dathan and Abiram, on account of their awful wickedness, were punished by removing them at once to eternal happiness. Ananias and Sapphira, for lying to the Holy Ghost, were sent immediately to heaven. Judas, on that principle, was rewarded for his treachery; while the disciples, for being faithful to their blessed master, fared incomparably worse than he, for they were left to toil and suffer many years on earth before they entered upon the reward that Judas received immediately after he hung himself.

I ask, candidly, if the doctrine of universal salvation does not render the criminal code of all nations, as well as the dealings of God, inconsistent with reason and common sense. All mankind concur in the belief that the punishment of death is of the severest kind that can be inflicted in this world; but if all go immediately to heaven when they die, it is a reward and not a punishment. No man is permitted to take his own life; but a court of justice in condemning a murderer to be hung, gives him permission to enter immediately into a state of happiness so great that it hath not even {55} entered into the mind of man to conceive its blessedness.*

[*It is obvious these arguments will not be felt by that class of Universalists who have gone to the extent of a denial of a future state of conscious existence after death. But it is supposed many who have drunk in the sentiment, still believe in a state of conscious existence beyond the grave. To this class the argument is legitimate and forcible.

It may here be observed that Universalism is a Proteus. It puts on every shape, and changes its form at every attack. This very fact ought to be regarded, by all persons of sense, as direct evidence of its fallacy. Truth never changes.

J.M.P.][4]

....

{98}

CHAPTER VI.
CONCLUDING REFLECTIONS.

The course dictated by common prudence.—The trail of the Serpent.—Duty of Christians.—Duty of Patriots in regard to the subject.

Now, friendly reader, you who have gone with me through this examination of the doctrine of Universal Salvation, what do you think of that creed? Is the proof of its truth so strong that it is utterly impossible that the doctrine can be false? Remember that the soul is of immense value, and its happiness ought not to be staked upon the truth of Universalism, unless proved true beyond the shadow of a doubt. Remember also, that if that doctrine is true you risk nothing by disbelieving it, but will be saved whether you believe it or not. Why then embrace a belief that does not even profess to render your salvation a particle more secure? But if you become a humble Christ- {99} ian, relying for pardon upon the blood of Jesus Christ, then will you be safe, in time and in eternity, whether Universalism prove true or false. The dictates of common prudence are sufficient to show the folly of running a fearful risk without a chance of gaining any thing by it, and running a risk when you might have pursued a perfectly safe course.

---

4. Editorial insertions by "J.M.P." are by John Mason Peck, who edited *The Serpent Uncoiled* and is the only name associated with it on the official title page.

If the doctrine of universal salvation is true, and all will be saved, why do they labor so hard to gain proselytes to that belief, and above all, why do they make such unceasing efforts to gain over to their side the members of evangelical churches? On these efforts to induce professors of religion to relinquish their belief in a future retribution, are plainly seen the slimy trail of the serpent.*

[* The wily SERPENT, snugly coiled up, and his shining scales glistening and dazzling the eyes of beholders, has been fully stretched out by the author, that his feculence and poisonous effluvia may be seen and known of all men. Doubtless he will writhe, and throw himself into violent contortions, but these pages show his PICTURE. And while it is our duty to manifest Christian charity, to the entire limits of the gospel, and exercise sincere sympathy for all *persons* who are blinded by such gross delusions, we can have no fellowship with the unfruitful works of darkness. They must be exposed, that they may be reproved.

J.M.P.] {100}

Let every Christian, who loves the cause of Christ and the souls of his fellow beings as he ought, use his influence to prevent the spread of this soul-destroying heresy.

No citizen of this Republic, who values the free institutions of this happy country, can wish to have a doctrine prevail whose tendency is to destroy the moral principles of those who embrace it, and to that extent strike a blow at our republican government.

Let every man, who wishes to keep the rights which our fathers, with the blessing of God, won for us—let every man who wishes to have these rights descend unimpaired to other generations—set his face like steel against every doctrine whose tendency it is to divest the minds of our countrymen of the fear of God. Should the day ever arrive, as it has done in France, when the people cease to believe that there is a God who will punish the villain whose crimes may escape human punishment, on that day the knell of our freedom will be rung, and here, as in France, a long night of despotism or anarchy will succeed.

Also available from
GREG KOFFORD BOOKS

Re-reading Job: Understanding the Ancient World's Greatest Poem

Michael Austin

Paperback, ISBN: 978-1-58958-667-3

Job is perhaps the most difficult to understand of all books in the Bible. Whil a cursory reading of the text seems to relay a simple story of a righteous ma whose love for God was tested through life's most difficult of challenges an rewarded for his faith through those trials, a closer reading of Job present something far more complex and challenging. The majority of the text is work of poetry that authors and artists through the centuries have recognize as being one of--if not the--greatest poem of the ancient world.

In *Re-reading Job: Understanding the Ancient World's Greatest Poem*, autho Michael Austin shows how most readers have largely misunderstood thi important work of scripture and provides insights that enable us to re-rea Job in a drastically new way. In doing so, he shows that the story of Job is fa more than that simple story of faith, trials, and blessings that we have all com to know, but is instead a subversive and complex work of scripture meant t inspire readers to rethink all that they thought they knew about God.

Praise for *Re-reading Job*:

"In this remarkable book, Michael Austin employs his considerable skil as a commentator to shed light on the most challenging text in the entir Hebrew Bible. Without question, readers will gain a deeper appreciation fo this extraordinary ancient work through Austin's learned analysis. Rereadin Job signifies that Latter-day Saints are entering a new age of mature biblic scholarship. It is an exciting time, and a thrilling work." — David Bokovo author, *Authoring the Old Testament*

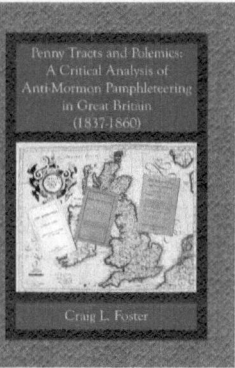

Penny Tracts and Polemics: A Critical Analysis of Anti-Mormon Pamphleteering in Great Britain, 1837–1860

Craig L. Foster

Hardcover, ISBN: 978-1-58958-005-3

By 1860, Mormonism had enjoyed a presence in Great Britain for over twenty years. Mormon missionaries experienced unprecedented success in conversions and many new converts had left Britain's shores for a new life and a new religion in the far western mountains of the American continent.

With the success of the Mormons came tales of duplicity, priestcraft, sexual seduction, and uninhibited depravity among the new religious adherents. Thousands of pamphlets were sold or given to the British populace as a way of discouraging people from joining the Mormon Church. Foster places the creation of these English anti-Mormon pamphlets in their historical context. He discusses the authors, the impact of the publications and the Mormon response. With illustrations and detailed bibliography.

Fire and Sword: A History of the Latter-day Saints in Northern Missouri, 1836-39

Leland Homer Gentry and Todd M. Compton

Hardcover, ISBN: 978-1-58958-103-6

Many Mormon dreams flourished in Missouri. So did many Mormon nightmare

The Missouri period—especially from the summer of 1838 when Josep took over vigorous, personal direction of this new Zion until the spring of 183 when he escaped after five months of imprisonment—represents a momer of intense crisis in Mormon history. Representing the greatest extreme of devotion and violence, commitment and intolerance, physical sufferin and terror—mobbings, battles, massacres, and political "knockdowns"— shadowed the Mormon psyche for a century.

Leland Gentry was the first to step beyond this disturbing period as a one sided symbol of religious persecution and move toward understanding it wit careful documentation and evenhanded analysis. In Fire and Sword, Tod Compton collaborates with Gentry to update this foundational work with fou decades of new scholarship, more insightful critical theory, and the wealth c resources that have become electronically available in the last few years.

Compton gives full credit to Leland Gentry's extraordinary achievemen particularly in documenting the existence of Danites and in attempting to te the Missourians' side of the story; but he also goes far beyond it, gracefull drawing into the dialogue signal interpretations written since Gentry an introducing the raw urgency of personal writings, eyewitness journalist and bemused politicians seesawing between human compassion and partisa harshness. In the lush Missouri landscape of the Mormon imagination whei Adam and Eve had walked out of the garden and where Adam would retur to preside over his posterity, the towering religious creativity of Joseph Smit and clash of religious stereotypes created a swift and traumatic frontier dram that changed the Church.

"Swell Suffering": A Biography of Maurine Whipple

Veda Tebbs Hale

Paperback, ISBN: 978-1-58958-124-1
Hardcover, ISBN: 978-1-58958-122-7

[Ma]urine Whipple, author of what some critics consider Mormonism's great-[es]t novel, *The Giant Joshua,* is an enigma. Her prize-winning novel has never [be]en out of print, and its portrayal of the founding of St. George draws on [he]r own family history to produce its unforgettable and candid portrait of [plu]ral marriage's challenges. Yet Maurine's life is full of contradictions and [un]answered questions. Veda Tebbs Hale, a personal friend of the paradoxical [no]velist, answers these questions with sympathy and tact, nailing each insight [do]wn with thorough research in Whipple's vast but under-utilized collected [pa]pers.

Praise for *"Swell Suffering"*:

"Hale achieves an admirable balance of compassion and objectivity to-[wa]rd an author who seemed fated to offend those who offered to love or be-[fri]end her. . . . Readers of this biography will be reminded that Whipple was a [ful]l peer of such Utah writers as Virginia Sorensen, Fawn Brodie, and Juanita [Br]ooks, all of whom achieved national fame for their literary and historical [wo]rks during the mid-twentieth century"
—Levi S. Peterson, author of *The Backslider* and *Juanita Brooks: Mormon [Hi]storian*

Excavating Mormon Pasts: The New Historiography of the Last Half Century

Newell G. Bringhurst and Lavina Fielding Anderson

Paperback, ISBN: 978-1-58958-115-9

Special Book Award - John Whitmer Historical Association

Mormonism was born less than 200 years ago, but in that short time it h
developed into a dynamic world religious movement. With that growth h
come the inevitable restructuring and reevaluation of its history and doctrir
Mormon and non-Mormon scholars alike have viewed Joseph Smit
religion as fertile soil for religious, historical and sociological studies. Ma
early attempts to either defend or defame the Church were at best sloppy a
often dishonest. It has taken decades for Mormon scholarship to mature
its present state. The editors of this book have assembled 16 essays addressi
the substantial number of published works in the field of Mormon stud
from 1950 to the present. The contributors come from various segments
the Mormon tradition and fairly represent the broad intellectual spectru
of that tradition. Each essay focuses on a particular aspect of Mormonis
(history, women's issues, polygamy, etc.), and each is careful to evenhandec
evaluate the strengths and weaknesses of the books under discussion. Mc
importantly, each volume is placed in context with other, related worl
giving the reader a panoramic view of contemporary research. Students
Mormonism will find this collection of historiographical essays an invaluat
addition to their libraries.

Mormon Polygamous Families:
Life in the Principle

Jessie L. Embry

Paperback, ISBN: 978-1-58958-098-5
Hardcover, ISBN: 978-1-58958-114-2

Mormons and non-Mormons all have their views about how polygamy was practiced in the Church of Jesus Christ of Latter-day Saints during the late nineteenth and early twentieth centuries. Embry has examined the participants themselves in order to understand how men and women living a nineteenth-century Victorian lifestyle adapted to polygamy. Based on records and oral histories with husbands, wives, and children who lived in Mormon polygamous households, this study explores the diverse experiences of individual families and stereotypes about polygamy. The interviews are in some cases the only sources of primary information on how plural families were organized. In addition, children from monogamous families who grew up during the same period were interviewed to form a comparison group. When carefully examined, most of the stereotypes about polygamous marriages do not hold true. In this work it becomes clear that Mormon polygamous families were not much different from Mormon monogamous families and non-Mormon families of the same era. Embry offers a new perspective on the Mormon practice of polygamy that enables readers to gain better understanding of Mormonism historically.

Joseph Smith's Polygamy, 3 Vols.

Brian Hales

Hardcover
Volume 1: History 978-1-58958-189-0
Volume 2: History 978-1-58958-548-5
Volume 3: Theology 978-1-58958-190-6

Perhaps the least understood part of Joseph Smith's life and teachings is his introduction of polygamy to the Saints in Nauvoo. Because of the persecution he knew it would bring, Joseph said little about it publicly and only taught it to his closest and most trusted friends and associates before his martyrdom.

In this three-volume work, Brian C. Hales provides the most comprehensive faithful examination of this much misunderstood period in LDS Church history. Drawing for the first time on every known account Hales helps us understand the history and teachings surrounding this secretive practice and also addresses and corrects many of the numerous allegations and misrepresentations concerning it. Hales further discusses how polygamy was practiced during this time and why so many of the early Saints were willing to participate in it.

Joseph Smith's Polygamy is an essential resource in understanding this challenging and misunderstood practice of early Mormonism.

Praise for *Joseph Smith's Polygamy*:

"Brian Hales wants to face up to every question, every problem, every fear about plural marriage. His answers may not satisfy everyone, but he gives readers the relevant sources where answers, if they exist, are to be found. There has never been a more thorough examination of the polygamy idea." —Richard L. Bushman, author of *Joseph Smith: Rough Stone Rolling*

"Hales's massive and well documented three volume examination of the history and theology of Mormon plural marriage, as introduced and practiced during the life of Joseph Smith, will now be the standard against which all other treatments of this important subject will be measured." —Danel W. Bachman, author of "A Study of the Mormon Practice of Plural Marriage before the Death of Joseph Smith"

A House for the Most High: The Story of the Original Nauvoo Temple

Matthew McBride

Hardcover, ISBN: 978-1-58958-016-9

This awe-inspiring book is a tribute to the perseverance of the human spirit. A House for the Most High is a groundbreaking work from beginning to end with its faithful and comprehensive documentation of the Nauvoo Temple's conception. The behind-the-scenes stories of those determined Saints involved in the great struggle to raise the sacred edifice bring a new appreciation to all readers. McBride's painstaking research now gives us access to valuable first-hand accounts that are drawn straight from the newspaper articles, private diaries, journals, and letters of the steadfast participants.

The opening of this volume gives the reader an extraordinary window into the early temple-building labors of the besieged Church of Jesus Christ of Latter-day Saints, the development of what would become temple-related doctrines in the decade prior to the Nauvoo era, and the 1839 advent of the Saints in Illinois. The main body of this fascinating history covers the significant years, starting from 1840, when this temple was first considered, to the temple's early destruction by a devastating natural disaster. A well-thought-out conclusion completes the epic by telling of the repurchase of the temple lot by the Church in 1937, the lot's excavation in 1962, and the grand announcement in 1999 that the temple would indeed be rebuilt. Also included are an astonishing appendix containing rare and fascinating eyewitness descriptions of the temple and a bibliography of all major source materials. Mormons and non-Mormons alike will discover, within the pages of this book, a true sense of wonder and gratitude for a determined people whose sole desire was to build a sacred and holy temple for the worship of their God.

The Man behind the Discourse: A Biography of King Follett

Joann Follett Mortensen

ISBN: 978-1-58958-036-7

Who was King Follett? When he was fatally injured digging a well i Nauvoo in March 1844, why did Joseph Smith use his death to deliver th monumental doctrinal sermon now known as the King Follett Discourse Much has been written about the sermon, but little about King.

Although King left no personal writings, Joann Follett Mortensen, King third great-granddaughter, draws on more than thirty years of research in civ ic and Church records and in the journals and letters of King's peers to piec together King's story from his birth in New Hampshire and moves westwar where, in Ohio, he and his wife, Louisa, made the life-shifting decision t accept the new Mormon religion.

From that point, this humble, hospitable, and hardworking family fo lowed the Church into Missouri where their devotion to Joseph Smith wa refined and burnished. King was the last Mormon prisoner in Missouri to b released from jail. According to family lore, King was one of the Prophet bodyguards. He was also a Danite, a Mason, and an officer in the Nauvo Legion. After his death, Louisa and their children settled in Iowa where som associated with the Cutlerities and the RLDS Church; others moved on t California. One son joined the Mormon Battalion and helped found Mo mon communities in Utah, Idaho, and Arizona.

While King would have died virtually unknown had his name not bee attached to the discourse, his life story reflects the reality of all those whos faith became the foundation for a new religion. His biography is more tha one man's life story. It is the history of the early Restoration itself.

Dead Wood and Rushing Water: Essays on Mormon Faith, Culture, and Family

Boyd Jay Petersen

Paperback, ISBN: 978-1-58958-658-1

r over a decade, Boyd Petersen has been an active voice in Mormon studies d thought. In essays that steer a course between apologetics and criticism, iving for the balance of what Eugene England once called the "radical ddle," he explores various aspects of Mormon life and culture—from the eam Mine near Salem, Utah, to the challenges that Latter-day Saints of the llennial generation face today.

aise for *Dead Wood and Rushing Water*:

"*Dead Wood and Rushing Water* gives us a reflective, striving, wise soul minating on his world. In the tradition of Eugene England, Petersen amines everything in his Mormon life from the gold plates to missions to eam mines to doubt and on to Glenn Beck, Hugh Nibley, and gender. It is ook I had trouble putting down." — Richard L. Bushman, author of *Joseph ith: Rough Stone Rolling*

"Boyd Petersen is correct when he says that Mormons have a deep hunger • personal stories—at least when they are as thoughtful and well-crafted as ꞓ ones he shares in this collection." — Jana Riess, author of *The Twible* and inking Sainthood

"Boyd Petersen invites us all to ponder anew the verities we hold, sharing in humility, tentativeness, and cheerful confidence that our paths will converge the end." — Terryl. L. Givens, author of *People of Paradox: A History of ormon Culture*

Hearken, O Ye People: The Historical Setting of Joseph Smith's Ohio Revelations

Mark Lyman Staker

Hardcover, ISBN: 978-1-58958-113-5

2010 Best Book Award - John Whitmer Historical Association

2011 Best Book Award - Mormon History Association

More of Mormonism's canonized revelations originated in or near Kirtla▮ than any other place. Yet many of the events connected with those revelations a▮ their 1830s historical context have faded over time. Mark Staker reconstru▮ the cultural experiences by which Kirtland's Latter-day Saints made sense of t▮ revelations Joseph Smith pronounced. This volume rebuilds that exciting deca▮ using clues from numerous archives, privately held records, museum collectio▮ and even the soil where early members planted corn and homes. From this v▮ array of sources he shapes a detailed narrative of weather, religious backgroun▮ dialect differences, race relations, theological discussions, food preparatio▮ frontier violence, astronomical phenomena, and myriad daily customs ▮ nineteenth-century life. The result is a "from the ground up" experience th▮ today's Latter-day Saints can all but walk into and touch.

Praise for *Hearken O Ye People*:

"I am not aware of a more deeply researched and richly contextualized stu▮ of any period of Mormon church history than Mark Staker's study of Mormo▮ in Ohio. We learn about everything from the details of Alexander Campbe▮ views on priesthood authority to the road conditions and weather on the fo▮ Lamanite missionaries' journey from New York to Ohio. All the Ohio revelatio▮ and even the First Vision are made to pulse with new meaning. This book set ▮ new standard of in-depth research in Latter-day Saint history."

-Richard Bushman, author of *Joseph Smith: Rough Stone Rollin▮*

"To be well-informed, any student of Latter-day Saint history and doctrine m▮ now be acquainted with the remarkable research of Mark Staker on the import▮ history of the church in the Kirtland, Ohio, area."

-Neal A. Maxwell Institute, Brigham Young University